TERRA'S PENGUINS

RAZIEL

RED
PENGUIN
Books

To Thomas M, who through his love and belief in me gave me the strength and courage to make this book possible.

CONTENTS

Introduction   vii

Prologue   1
1. MICHAEL   9
2. GABRIEL   29
3. RAPHAEL   47
4. JOPHIEL   59
5. URIEL   73
6. HANAEL   91

Acknowledgments   109
About the Author   111

INTRODUCTION

Divine Intervention - a revelation that is the only explanation I can provide for the developments of this story.

While gazing over a quarry from a picture window, I saw three structures that resembled six-foot penguins and a strong force entered my thoughts and commanded me to write a story of three aliens from another solar system that are shaped like earth penguins that are sent here to save our planet from self-destruction. They metamorphose into humans and each is brought up in a different country and they reunite and bring brotherhood to the world. I fought this tooth and nail and argued I am not a writer. The response was always to have faith and the help I would need will be there.

I prayed for the guidance I would need and the messages were strong preparing my manuscript. Researching a book by Taylor Caldwell titled "Dialogues With The Devil" for information on my book, strange occurrences took place. Example: doors opening and closing by themselves and lights blinking off for no logical explanation. Whenever I left this book for a friend or relative to test it out, the same thing happened to them. I attribute these phenomenal observations to Lucifer trying to prevent this information out into our world. The book by Taylor Caldwell is a conversation between Lucifer and Saint Michael the Archangel. Information Satan would never want out in this world because he is the last one to cast a vote for brotherhood of man.

I know he is the Devil and portrayed as a magician in my book and believe me, he is for real.

The Planet Terra (which is Earth) has completed over 2,000 full rotations around its Sun since the last ray of hope was sent there to help keep them from destroying each other.

During that time, many cultures, kingdoms and governments have taken on numerous changes. Terra's inhabitants are striving for survival. The planet is in turmoil. It is the youngest of all the 400 billion galaxies in the vast Universe. The Creator made all the Planets in perfection—only this one fell and became diseased. The inhabitants were influenced by greed, and only a few have tried in vain to educate themselves on love; these were laughed at as being weak. Was there any hope for these poor creatures who would destroy themselves by a nuclear disaster if something drastic was not done?

This is a love story of six families. Six penguin aliens from another Solar System volunteer to study and possibly save the humans who occupy the Planet Terra. The other 400 billion galaxies live as a peaceful, universal family. Will the self-destruction of Terra be stopped by these wonderful aliens who will disguise themselves as humans? Will Lucifer, the main vein of evil there, terminate them before their task is complete?

*I increased my main characters from three to six because I wanted to reach out globally for a brotherhood of man.

PROLOGUE

he Planet Pellisa, from the most advanced solar system, has a pink and lime green sky. It has sandy beaches that are pure white with gold shimmers speckled throughout. Her waters are violet and so clear that the bottom of her oceans are visible from the deepest point. The mountains are aqua and gold, contrasting with trees of bright crimson. Her grass floor is a mixture of all colors; a rainbow in her sky looks like a reflection from this velvety cloak. Pellisa's rivers and streams are purely silver with lilac crests; her lakes are scented lavender sweet. Her climate is mild with gently flowing air, fragrant with the scent of fruit trees, fields of flowers yet unnamed, and dewy turf. Her sun, which they call Tau Ceti, is a great lavender prism turning on its axis. Pellisa is the most magnificent of all the planets in the Universe.

Pellisa's inhabitants are penguin-like in shape. They have a thick pure white fur with a gold trim. Their intelligence is difficult to equate, being 400 billion years more advanced than Terra (Earth). They have never been exposed to death or sin. Perfect in the eyes of their Creator, these penguins swim with their wings under the lavender seas. No greed, lust, or disease has touched these magnificent creatures. All their homage to family, work, play, art, and all culture is offered to their Creator's intentions. The Creator's Presence on their planet is as familiar to them as the scent of their flowers. He communicates with them daily, as does a father with his family. The inhabitants of Pellisa often ask their Creator about the billions of other stars, and if other life existed in our great Universe. The Creator's response was always the same. His response was, "There are 400 billion other solar systems in our great Universe, and Pellisa was the very first created. All the other inhabited planets are much younger and less beautiful. They are the most advanced and gifted of all and they and all the Universe were created in perfect harmony."

The eldest of the inhabitants of Pellisa was named Hewaer; he was known as the wisest penguin, and all the others came to him for advice. One evening they were all gathered in the domed meeting hall when the Creator appeared. They asked again of other species and if other life existed in the great Universe. Hewaer was curious as to the youngest solar system, since theirs was the oldest. He asked the Creator to explain the inhabitants of the youngest planet. The Creator spoke to them for the first time in detail of another solar system and the species that live there. He said, "The youngest solar system has a sun with ten heavenly bodies that revolve around it. There is only one planet with life, and the inhabitants there are referred to as human beings. They were created in the image and likeness of Myself, but through time many have become their own worst enemy."

Hewaer and the rest were all confused about the word enemy and asked the Creator for the definition. He answered, "Some of these human beings harbor malicious intent towards their brothers, and they may destroy each other if something does not change their way of life. Humanity is a group of infinitely powerful creatures. My Spirit is inside of them and this enlightens and enlivens their lives, if they would only realize this. All of them have the Spirit of their Creator within them and they are all the same, none better or worse. Realization of this fact would change them to reach out and help each other so none would starve or go unloved."

Hewaer asked if there was anything they could do to help these lost and unhappy creatures called humans. The Creator answered, "If you wish to sacrifice an offspring, and send him or her to Terra to possibly teach them to believe and trust in Me, and to love each other the way I love them, they will have another chance of redeeming themselves. It is their own free will." There was silence in the room and all were in deep thought. Hewaer's daughter Nacrecia was due for her first penguin male in two weeks. She asked her husband Revour if they should make the sacrifice to send their infant penguin to Terra. Revour replied, "The Creator will see that our first infant will grow up on Terra soil and teach all the human family what he knows here on Pellisa, and hopefully he will return to us unharmed and enlightened by his bravery and sacrifice."

Two weeks passed and Nacrecia was going into labor. She bore one male offspring and there was a stillness in the air, and her breathing stopped, then started heavily again – another birth, only so unexpected and identical to the first male penguin. Nacrecia then began gasping for another breath, totally in shock when the third, fourth, fifth and sixth males were born. No one said a word; silence was all she heard. Then Nacrecia's husband Revour spoke, "Our six children are born so they can be sent by us for the Creator's purpose to bring peace to the Planet Terra." Nacrecia gazed into the eyes of all six male babies, and there was an aura about them; she felt so overwhelmed by love. Tear after tear ran down her cheek and she placed all six of them around her and prayed for the Creator to watch over them. She did not leave their side until it was time for their journey to Terra.

The day finally came for the children to leave and all were gathered in the meeting hall for the final farewells. The Creator suddenly appeared and the radiant light surrounded the penguin children. He spoke to them, "Your mission on Terra is very close at hand; you may refrain from this dangerous journey if you so desire." They all looked at one another. They then replied, "It will please our Creator to have these humans love one another, and, if we can be used to help them, we will try our best to be instrumental in bringing them brotherhood."

Then down from the ceiling came rays of white light, brighter than the sun Tau Ceti, and they landed around all six of them. The Creator spoke, "Take these gold rings and place them to your hearts. They will remain there until you metamorphose into human beings, at which time you will be placed accordingly in your new human physical bodies. This symbol of the magic ring will have the power to subdue all demons. Always keep it on your new body, for the power of it will bring all of you protection when needed. Your pilgrimage to Terra will deliver you to six different countries. Each of you will live with a family in that given country, then unite when you mature into adults, and hopefully you will prove that all may live as one loving family on Terra. MICHAEL will be American and live in the United States of America, GABRIEL will be Hebrew and live in Israel, RAPHAEL will be Russian and live in Russia, JOPHIEL will be Muslim and live in Palestine, URIEL will be Hispanic and live in Spain, and HANAEL will be Chinese and live in China."

All the inhabitants of Pellisa gathered around the spaceship to see the children's takeoff to the unknown planet of Terra. The ship was shaped similar to a six-pointed star. Each enormous point was a cabin equipped to house one of them comfortably for flight. Not knowing what to expect, they climbed into their designated chambers, which were furnished to keep them alive while still in penguin form.

The journey to Terra was a trillion light years from Pellisa. As the silver ship began to take off, the Pellisa inhabitants all held wings and watched the huge star-shaped ship advance higher and higher until it disappeared completely through the pink and lime green sky.

The ship started to direct itself through the huge masses of galaxies, one always more intriguing than the next. They watched shooting stars and comets soar across the skies, the magnificent Universe passing their enormous window view.

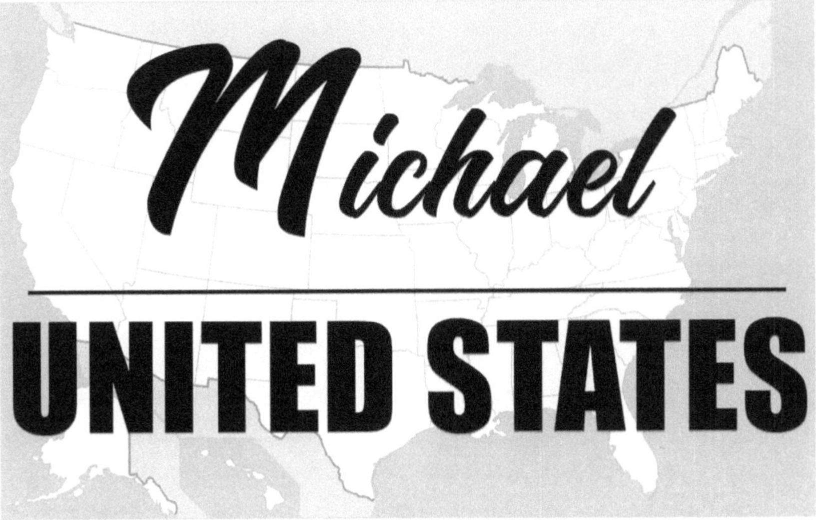
Michael
UNITED STATES

Chapter One

MICHAEL

As the first penguin child born to Nacrecia sat in his rocket cabin with his eyes closed, he anticipated the uncertain events to come. He felt his heart for the ring the Creator had given all six of them. He looked at it inquisitively, not knowing what the word meant in the center of the ring. It was engraved with the name Michael. He assumed it was his newly acquired name. Although the Creator mentioned six names, and where each child would live, they were not sure which specific name was given to each of them. Michael was the name given to the first born, and now he knew he was headed to live in the United States of America. As Michael came closer to his landing destination, he began to feel different.

Metamorphosis was setting in and his insides began changing first. His lungs felt like they were closing and he realized that he, for the first time, could stay out of water without discomfort. He breathed deeply and felt that, whatever form he was taking, it was necessary for completion of his mission. Under the spacesuit, he felt chilled, not realizing his fur was being replaced by human skin. His wings formed arms and hands and his webbed feet took on the human form. He reached up and removed the helmet to his suit and it was then that he saw his human arm and hand. He thought it did not belong to him—he never saw such a thing. He moved his index finger up and down slowly for a minute and then finally realized he was controlling it. He jumped up and proceeded to feel his head. He felt for his beak and kept grabbing in thin air at nothing. He slowly came in closer with his newly formed hand to feel for his beak and finally caught his reflection in the window. He thought it was an alien. He lifted his arm and touched the top of his head. The alien did the same movement. He started believing this alien was somewhat friendly, so he walked to the window and pressed his face against it. His breath made a steam mark on the window and he wiped it with his hand. His alien friend did the same thing and at that moment he realized it was his own reflection.

Michael's new form was indeed human. He had golden hair, a manly smiling face and blue eyes. He was 17 years old by Terra years. His body was well built and masculine. He was quite handsome by human standards. Michael climbed back into the landing chair and looked straight ahead. He relaxed for the landing only moments away.

As the six-pointed spacecraft neared Terra's atmosphere, it resembled a huge shooting star. It zoomed in for Michael to be released from his cabin. It was a snowy night. The exit door opened and he could see lights as he parachuted into the icy cold night. He saw a huge white building zooming in front of his descent. He closed his eyes for the impact he was about to make. Michael crashed into the roof by force, leaving his eyes burning, causing him to experience pain. He had landed on the roof of a Supreme Court Justice, a close friend of the President of the United States. Justice Jude Moroni was peacefully smoking his pipe by the fireplace in his office library when he heard a disturbance. Snow was falling and the house lawn was completely covered. Judge Moroni thought the fireplace wood was crackling from the intense heat until he heard moans. He looked out of his office window and saw someone lying on the roof. The Judge called for the servants to bring blankets, then wrapped Michael's naked body warmly and called for an ambulance.

When Michael opened his eyes for the first time on Terra, Judge Moroni was holding his head and rubbing his shoulder. Michael felt comforted and sensed he was going to be okay. Arriving at the hospital in five minutes, the emergency room attendants ran through the snow and picked up Michael's stretcher. When Michael opened his eyes again, he saw nothing but black. He panicked and fell into a deep sleep.

Michael was unconscious for two days. During this time, he especially intrigued the nurse's aide assigned to his room. She was still in training and found herself lured to him like a magnet. She would slip into his room a few times an hour. Stephanie was eighteen years old. Her hair was golden blonde. She had the widest blue eyes and, when she looked at you, the radiance from her beauty shined all around her.

Michael began to moan. He slowly moved his hands up to the bandages on his eyes. He thought this was the end of the journey and that he probably would never function properly again. Judge Moroni called for Stephanie. She ran frantically through the hallway as fast as she could and, when she entered Michael's room, she felt her heart pounding so fiercely she thought she might pass out. She forgot that, in case of consciousness, she was to call the doctor on duty. She proceeded to unwrap the head bandages so quickly that one swoop unraveled the gauze and Michael's eyes saw Stephanie's eyes first. They gazed in wonder into each other's eyes. Michael had been holding Judge Moroni's hand and let it go. He reached for Stephanie and asked where he was. Stephanie sat on the bed, never taking her eyes off the most handsome boy she had ever seen. When Stephanie asked Michael where he hurt, he said he was so relieved to have his eyesight back that everything felt good.

Judge Moroni asked Stephanie to call in the physician. When Stephanie left the room, Judge Moroni asked Michael where he lived. Michael said he did not know. His past was a complete blank. The Judge asked Michael if he wanted to come home with him until his memory came back. Michael felt warmed and secure looking into Judge Moroni's face. The Judge's frame was tall and thin with a curly head of salt and pepper hair. Michael took Judge Moroni's hand and thanked him. He then knew this was the Creator's plan for him on Terra. The Judge invited Stephanie to his home for a celebration dinner to honor Michael's recovery.

Arriving home, Judge Moroni had forgotten to inform his wife, Angela, of their new guest. Angela Moroni stared at the pair. She was taken back by her husband's attention to Michael. The Judge introduced Michael to his wife. She sat down and looked at Michael. She felt so much warmth and goodness radiating about him that she proceeded to hug and kiss this boy whom she knew nothing about. The Moroni's were never blessed with children. Angela went upstairs and prepared the guest room for Michael. He had no suitcase, no identification, and she had no idea where he was from. He only told them his name was Michael. Angela happily planned a clothes shopping trip.

The Judge asked Angela to call their magician friend, David Penn, and to invite him to their home on Saturday for a dinner in honor of Michael. David Penn always accepted Judge Moroni's invitations because the Judge provided David with entrance visas to any country in which he wished to perform his astounding magic tricks. He has been known to walk through pyramids in Egypt, make buildings in New York disappear, and fly over the Grand Canyon with nothing attached to his body, or so it seemed. He is the most exalted celebrity in his field in the world.

Stephanie Shannacy telephoned the Moroni home as she was

invited to do. Angela answered the phone. Stephanie again found it hard to speak. She felt a lump in her throat. Michael was summoned to the phone. Never having spoken on the phone before, he did not know how to hold the receiver. Angela saw he was nervous and placed the phone to his ear. Stephanie waited for a hello, which Michael did not know he was supposed to say. Michael cleared his throat and Stephanie then knew he was on the other end. She said, "Michael, is that you?" Michael replied, "Stephanie?" She swallowed hard and asked him how he was feeling. They spoke to each other as if they were afraid of some unknown goose-bumps each were experiencing. Stephanie asked Michael if he wanted to go into Center City for some fun. He accepted, not knowing what she was talking about, but, if she was going, it had to be exciting. When Angela found out that Stephanie was picking up Michael, she gave him her major credit cards and told him to buy all the clothes he needed. He looked at the card and looked at Judge Moroni's striped pajamas, which he had been wearing since they removed the hospital gown.

Angela gave Michael her husband's jeans, shirt and shoes so Michael could wear them until he bought clothes. Michael looked in the mirror at his new form. It was so different from his real body. The clothes had to be put on and he knew nothing about how they fit. He took the shirt first and remembered Judge Moroni had his round plastic things coming down the front. He placed the shirt on and then looked at the undershirt. Where did it go? He placed it over his shirt, and, looking in the mirror, he thought it was right. He put the jeans on with the zipper in the back. He put the boxer shorts on over the jeans. He knew something was wrong. He called Angela and she did not answer. He put his shoes on and looked at the socks. They looked so funny. He figured he would ask Angela where they were to go and proceeded to walk downstairs. To his amazement, Angela and Stephanie were sitting in the living room. His appearance was so incredibly humorous, they thought he was clowning. They both laughed. Michael sat on the chair and looked at them smiling. Angela said, "Michael, you have a great sense of humor. Stephanie and I really enjoyed that laugh." Stephanie told Michael that Angela wanted her to take him to the mall for some clothes. Michael said it was fine and got up to head for the door. Stephanie asked, "Michael, don't you have to remove some things?" "What things?" he asked. Angela told Michael to put her husband's coat on and also his hat. She noticed the socks were still in his hand, so as not to embarrass him, she took her husband's snow boots out of the closet and told Michael that he needed to put them on. He looked at them funny. Angela told him to remove his shoes and place the socks on, then the boots. Stephanie just watched in amusement.

As Stephanie started her car to pull out of the driveway, Michael could not help but wonder how odd this vehicle was, compared to how transportation was on Pellisa. Then he quickly remembered how Pellisa was the first created of all planets and Terra was the last. It was only natural that they were so primitive, being billions of years less advanced.

When they started driving towards the mall, Michael was in awe of the crowds and automobiles in the parking lot. All the people were rushing and honking horns, trying to get somewhere so quickly. They parked near the entrance and proceeded to enter the mall. The first store they came to was a popular teen clothing store. Upon entering, the salesman walked over and asked Michael his size. Michael just looked at him with a blank stare. Stephanie said he must be about a 32 inch waist. He picked up three different pairs of jeans in a size 32 and handed them to Michael. Stephanie proceeded to look at the shirts. She picked out three denim shirts and told Michael to take off his overcoat so she could look at his shoulders to see if he was a medium or large. He removed his overcoat. The customers roared with laughter. Michael started to laugh himself, not knowing it was mockery. Stephanie was mortified. She knew that Michael had no idea what was happening. Without hesitation, Stephanie took the salesman aside and asked him to provide Michael with a wardrobe that was similar to what he himself would buy. She told him to provide Michael with all the accessories he would need to complete at least seven outfits. She told the salesman that Michael had a loss of memory and asked him to not make him feel out of place. The salesman took Michael not into the dressing room but into the office, which was far more private. He clothed him with everything from hats to scarves and socks and gloves and coats. He watched Michael with each new look get more handsome, and, from the look in Michael's eyes, the salesman thought this guy must be very intriguing. He handed Michael his business card and told him that if he needed assistance in the future he would be happy to help out.

Michael left the store in one of the newly bought outfits. They stopped at a shoe store and Michael tried on boots and sneakers, which he purchased. They let Michael wear his sneakers home. He took his newly bought socks and placed them on his feet. Michael thought how odd this was—to cover one's whole body with cloth. He laughed to himself, recalling to mind his beautiful fur skin on Pellisa. They left the mall and headed for Stephanie's car in the parking lot. They made a fantastic looking couple.

Walking towards Stephanie's car in the mall parking lot, they noticed a gang of boys all dressed the same. They were around sixteen years old, all wearing black, including black headbands. Stephanie was panic-stricken. She knew carjacking was so prevalent in the area, and she was positive trouble was facing them. She went into her handbag for her container of mace. She fumbled around frantically until she felt the slim tin. Holding it under her arm, she shook like a leaf walking near this gang of five. Without warning, one of them walked closely in back of them to see what car they were going to. When they got to her white convertible, the gang member reached out and snatched Stephanie's purse. Michael never saw violence and therefore did not know this was a dangerous situation. Stephanie watched as he pulled her keys out of her purse. He told her to open the car door. She did so, and then he told them both to get inside. Stephanie refused. He took his fist and punched her in the jaw. It was when she cried out in pain that Michael realized they were being attacked. He turned around to all five of them and said that, if they wanted to live, they had better not make another move. All five laughed at him and started coming towards him. Stephanie was lying on the ground, screaming for Michael to run. Michael remembered the ring the Creator had given him and his brothers in times of trouble, which was on his finger, and proceeded to rub it. In a matter of seconds, Michael was transformed into a fierce warrior. His body took on the penguin wings and his muscles, from head to toe, increased rapidly. He flapped his wings once, and elevated about two feet off the ground. The gang members were paralyzed with fear. Michael picked up the boy who hit Stephanie and carried him over to where she lay. Michael told him to help her up. The boy held out his hand for Stephanie to hold. Looking at Michael's eyes, she held out her hand. Michael watched closely as the gang member helped Stephanie to her feet. Michael asked the boy why he would hit a girl and why he would want to take property that did not belong to him. The boy said she was no different than anyone and he would steal anything he wanted because he had no other means of support. Michael asked him if he would steal from his family. The boy said he had no family. Michael lined all of them up next to the car. He challenged each one to a fight. No one budged. He told them that if they did not follow his orders they would pay the consequences. He told the boy who hit Stephanie to apologize. The boy knew he was either going to apologize or risk being hurt. He mimicked the apology, for fear of embarrassment in front of his friends, and kneeled down on one knee and said he was sorry. Michael told him that, if he sees him again in this kind of situation, the consequences were going to be severe. He told him and his friends to go back to school and get an education and, if they wanted to be in a gang, to start one that would prevent crime and murders on the streets of Washington. With that statement, Michael returned to his human state. Then he and Stephanie got into her car and headed home.

Stephanie was in a state of shock. She kept picturing Michael in his warrior form: wings spread ten feet across; hovering two feet off the ground. She thought she must have been dreaming. With all her courage she asked him where he came from. He took her by the hand and said that, if he were to tell her, she could not reveal his secret to anyone. She agreed. He told her of his home on Pellisa and how everyone lived without fear or hate. He told her of his pilgrimage to Terra and how he and his five brothers were sent by the Creator to bring her planet peace and love and to help them from destroying one another. She listened in awe, believing every word to be true.

When they arrived home, Stephanie escorted Michael into the living room. Angela Moroni could not believe how handsome Michael looked in his new attire. She invited Stephanie to a welcoming party for Michael next Saturday evening. Stephanie accepted eagerly, not thinking of her work schedule or anything else, except the fact she was falling in love with someone who was not of her planet.

The following day Michael was invited to go on a tour with the judge to see the White House. Since the Judge knew everyone in the Cabinet, including the President, on a personal basis, Michael was in for a real interesting visit. The first person Michael came into contact with was the General of the United States Army. He was in full uniform, with medals expanding from the center of his chest all the way across to his forearm. General O'Donnell was the military's wisest leader. He had a wisdom and aura that commanded respect. The general asked Michael what his plans were for the future. The

Judge explained the situation and that Michael was still suffering from amnesia. The General asked Michael to consider a military career, since he was at an age where he could enlist into a military academy and climb to high ranks. Michael said he was not sure yet what his future would be, but he would consider the service. The Judge and the General took Michael into the private quarters of the Oval Office where the President was holding a meeting for the dignitaries of four other nations with regards to how much nuclear power was distributed throughout the world. They waited in the outer office, and the staff was surprised to see a boy with these two powerful men.

Michael, the Judge and the General were summoned into the Oval Office of the President. Michael reached out his hand and was surprised the President was of a different color. President Williams was the first elected black President. The judge said, "Mr. President, please meet my new family addition, Michael." The President asked all three to be seated. The President said, "Perhaps you and I can get to know each other better. Let's get you working on a special private project of mine called "Universal Youth Core" which, in detail, is uniting all the youth in all the countries of Terra to form a club to better the planet and bring about an understanding of all our differences so we can learn to respect and love one another." Michael was thrilled. He looked at Judge Moroni and asked, "Judge, may I be a part of the President's project?" The Judge said yes, and Michael thanked the President for his appointment. The President told Michael to contact all the American Ambassadors to arrange an appointment with the youths of the designated countries, as to form a club so large that everyone on Terra would recognize a member of the Universal Youth Core. Then they went into a formal dining room and had lunch served to them. They joked and laughed at Michael's innocence. Michael was to report the next day for his first day of work on his new project. He went by the name

Michael Moroni. All the staff thought Michael was the Judge's nephew.

Saturday morning arrived and Angela was scurrying around getting ready for Michael's party that evening. She invited forty dignitaries from several countries, several of the White House staff, and the President himself. She called Stephanie and told her to bring some friends with her. She told David Penn, the magician, to think of a magical trick just for Michael. The magician told Angela he would perform his best trick as of yet and dedicate it to Michael. Angela was ecstatic.

Angela set the library up as a showroom. The main area where David would perform was in front of their wall-sized fireplace. All the chairs were turned, facing that area. Angela had several lighting technicians from the nearby theatre place the proper lighting for the magical effects. She had five butlers serving appetizers and the main dining room table filled with delectable food specialties from around the world. She hired a rock band to play in the recreation room for all the younger people. Everything seemed to be in order. In just a few hours, Michael's party would begin.

In the private townhouse of David Penn, in the quiet town of Georgetown, the magician paced frantically in his living room. His butler and confidant, an Englishman named George White, watched him with a certain fear, for he knew from past experiences with David that his anger could bring on a diabolical consequence. David told George that, as of last week, a force was placed on Terra that was so strong he could hardly think. He said that, as of one week ago, his memory has not been clear. He said there is a force so strong it could be used to read the minds of evil men and negate their destructive intent. David was furious. He placed his black cape over his back and paced the floor with a demeanor his butler friend had never seen before. David's hazel eyes grew a piercing black, his skin turned a gray color, and his order to the butler was even more frightening. "Bring to me all the famous psychics in the

area. I must find the source of this power; it will be destroyed."
Fury flashed in his eyes. The frightened butler secretly packed his
luggage and took the first flight home to England.

Michael began dressing for the party. He put on a white wool
double breasted suit. His long blonde hair was to his shoulders, so
Angela put it in a ponytail. He looked like a movie star. All the
guests waited for Michael to come down the wide spiral staircase for
his grand appearance.

Michael came down the stars slowly, surprised to see Stephanie
looking up the stairway with so much excitement and anticipation.
She ran to greet him. She wore a plain white wool mini dress with a
pearl choker and pearl earrings. This combination, with her
platinum blonde hair, made her look angelic. They walked together
into the greeting area where all Judge Jude's political associates were
gathered in a greeting line. The President himself was there,
speaking with Judge Jude, when Michael approached them. The
President kissed Michael on the cheek and told him this evening he
could start making connections for his next project, "Universal
Youth Core," since delegates from around Terra were present.

Michael met delegates from Israel, China, Palestine, Spain and
Russia. He told all five delegates he would be visiting their countries
to organize the Youth Core so a universal understanding and
sharing could be established with the younger generations on Terra.
They thought the idea was brilliant.

The band was playing in the recreation room and all the
younger people were gathered around, enjoying the rock band that
was well known throughout the United States. This was all so new
to Michael. He watched as Stephanie swayed back and forth and
moved her head up and down. She grabbed his hands and started
rocking him back and forth. Then she took him to the middle of
the floor. They twisted around so fast that they both fell into the
nearby sofa. The leader of the band asked Michael to come up to
the platform and handed him the mic. Michael had no idea what to

say. He started thanking everyone for coming to his party. He announced that he was heading a Universal Youth Core for the purpose of spreading love and peace through Terra. As he was speaking to the crowded room, he felt all around him a great support system. They clapped loudly and all cheered him for his vision of all youths coming together as one family on Terra.

David, the magician, was driving over to the Moroni home when he began feeling the force again. It was getting stronger as he came closer to his destination. He could not believe it. This force was in the Moroni home. He walked up the driveway and, by the time he arrived at the front door, he was in a total sweat. This, he thought, could not happen. He knew he was in trouble.

David entered the home and, to him, the house was like a heart, beating faster and faster. The walls seemed to throb back and forth. He asked the butler for a glass of water and sat down in the foyer. He was hyperventilating more than he had ever experienced. Angela greeted David with a hug and kiss and asked him if he needed anything before his appearance in the library. David said his trick needed no equipment, that it was a form of hypnosis. Angela said she could not wait to see the performance.

All the guests filed into the library, wondering what was to take place. Michael, Stephanie, the President, Judge Moroni and Angela all faced the platform. The lights were lowered and, although there was no rear door, David appeared as if out of thin air. His black silky hair flowed long to his shoulders, his hazel eyes stalwart as an eagles, his smile easy and unassuming, and his tightly muscled chest visible above a plunging neckline. His six foot, four-inch frame was draped all in black, baggy pants, with a loosely fitted tuxedo jacket, waist length, over a body hugging muscle shirt. His coloring a flawless tan, a perfect blend of vibrant copper, coral and deep peach. He resembled a Greek God. Everyone present stood up and gave him a standing ovation. The entire room was ecstatic with anticipation of David's performance. David, with his impeccable manners, welcomed Michael and said he was dedicating the performance to Judge Moroni's soon to be adopted son.

David asked Stephanie to step up to the platform. He joked with her for a few minutes, then asked her to look him in the eyes. When she did, she noticed there was smoke the color of aqua circling them. She stood in front of the crowd and somehow was transformed into a body looking exactly like that of David. David asked her how she felt. She answered in his voice. Everyone was in awe. Michael was feeling very nervous. Where was she? How could he possibly clone himself? It was so astounding, and everyone held their breath. Then David asked Stephanie if she could fly. She said, in his voice, "Like a bird." He commanded, "Take flight, Stephanie." She spread her arms and her body lifted off the floor; she flew around the ceiling for five minutes, and everyone gasped for their breath, it was so spectacular. When she landed back on the platform, David said to her, "You can go back to being Stephanie now." She immediately took on her own form again. The audience was in a state of shock. David then motioned for Michael to come up on the platform.

The lights in the library were darkened and Michael stood face to face with David. David asked Michael to look him in the eyes and then remembered where he came from. Michael followed David's wish and proceeded to stare hard into the hazel eyes of David. Michael saw a vast power beyond his imagination. Michael reversed the hypnosis and asked David where he was from, never breaking his eye contact. David felt his body go into a deep sweat. He felt a force he never did before. Unable to break from Michael's glance, he took on his true satanic form. The first change was his eyes, from hazel to piercing black, then his skin turned gray, and then horns protruded from the back of his head. He felt his shoes pop off his feet when his huge hoofs grew out from his legs. He was absolutely terrifying for all to see. Michael asked David, "Who are you?" David answered, "Now or in my past?" Michael replied, "In your past." David said, "I was Lucifer, the greatest Archangel in Heaven." Then David started changing form again, only this time his golden-shod feet twinkled with the energy of his being and barely touched the floor. He was beautiful beyond all imagining, he who once had been the viceroy of the Creator, the greatest and noblest and proudest Archangel of them all, and was dearly beloved of his Father and brothers. Once the ambassador to angels, who stood at the hand of the Creator, where no one equaled him for splendor and majesty and regal demeanor. His large white hands shone with gems, which blazed to the prismatic light of the sun, shining vibrantly through the large stained glass windows in the library. His upper arms were girdled with bands of jeweled gold and were muscular and strong. The audience thought all this was an act. Only Michael knew different. "Who are you now, David?" Michael asked. David turned again into the horrifying satanic form. Michael asked him why he was so great, and now so small. He answered, "I did not torture my brother angels the way you humans here on Terra torture their brothers. Jealousy and lust are all you humans know. How to starve your brothers so yourselves can have more wealth. None of you are worth the dirt on the heels of my feet. Yet the Creator loves you humans the most; I cannot justify or understand it. I cannot forgive Him for loving all of you. He wants me to repent and agree with Him that you are deserving of His love. I will remain here to tempt you until you destroy yourselves. The Creator will forgive me when He sees the nuclear warheads released and all mankind destroyed. I only tempt; you humans are weak by nature and will prove in the long run that I am right. I will laugh with joy when Terra is nothing but a smoldering ember."

Michael took his eyes off David for fear that he would question his own identity. David reverted back to being himself. He grabbed Michael's arm and, spinning him around for eye contact, asked, "Who are you, Michael?" Glancing quickly at David, Michael was locked into a stare. He trembled as he tried in vain to break away,

Michael knew his own identity would be revealed and was terrified. Michael felt his body tremble as his clothes started to bulge from the fur growing on his body. His webbed feet popped out of his shoes and socks, his arms became thin, membranous extensions, and then they were covered with his white and gold fur. His beak protruded from his nose and his white fur breast popped out of his shirt. He stood in front of his guests in full penguin form. Everyone laughed and cheered, believing this to be part of a magical trick. Michael held the gold ring in his hand and began praying the Creator would come to his rescue. He rubbed the ring and suddenly began to speak, "I am from the planet Pellisa, and I have come here with my brothers to help spread love and brotherhood to all humankind. Look up at the ceiling and the Creator will show you why." Everyone bent their head backwards and faced the ceiling. The huge chandelier started to shake. The light inside was brighter than the sun. The guests were in a trance. The voice of the Creator then filled the library. There were angels hovering around the chandelier and looking down on all the guests. The voice then said, "My planet Pellisa is my greatest of all, yet this small creature and his brothers risked their lives to help my children on Terra understand that love is the answer to all their problems. I sent them to teach my children on Terra the true meaning of love and many of them will take this message into their hearts. It is my decision to let them have the free will to decide.

"Why you, Lucifer, had it all. You were the most beautiful of my creations, and yet you wanted all my power." David watched as Michael metamorphosed back to a physical human being. David looked up at the ceiling, saying, "You are the Creator of Heaven and all the galaxies. You are the Holy One. Why do you waste your time on these creatures that hurt you? Soon they will destroy themselves with a nuclear war, with weapons you gave them the intelligence to make. Not until that day, when they completely destroy themselves by their own evil ways – maliciousness and ignorance – will I worship you again. Give up hope for these you call your loved ones, take home your messengers from Pellisa, and I will certainly bow down before you." The Creator answered, "Until you learn to love all your universal brothers, Lucifer, there can be no healing for you."

The chandelier became dim again and the platform was the same as before. Michael and David looked like they did before the performance, and both just looked at the audience. The President stood up and clapped for them and all the others followed. A standing ovation for something that was so miraculous, and yet all thought of it as a magical trick of some sort.

The President shook Michael's hand and asked him if he would organize his Youth Core next week and to visit a country of his choice. Michael agreed, wondering, where were my brothers now? Were they all safe? Michael asked the President if he could go to the United Nations to meet all the heads of government, hopeful he would find out the whereabouts of his five brothers. The President told him it would be arranged next week. Michael walked over to Stephanie. She hugged him closely and said how proud she was to be a part of this great historical event.

Gabriel

ISRAEL

Chapter Two

GABRIEL

The Pellisa spaceship now had five Pellisa "children" to deliver to Terra. The ship started to point herself toward Israel. Gabriel was awakened by a strange feeling. His breathing was somehow different. He felt his chest heaving in and out at a rapid pace. He sensed his air was being pulled out of his stomach, rather than from his lungs. He felt his chest and there was no fur. Gabriel panicked. He looked down at his chest and the vision of his newly formed human physical body was extremely alarming, but Gabriel realized his new form was necessary for his mission. He looked at his newly formed feet and glared at the difference from his webbed ones. How could he balance himself on these bony structures with those wiggly fatty things protruding from them? He stood up and wobbled back and forth. He was without fur, and he had no idea this was not the normal way to go in public.

It was Gabriel's turn now. In an instant the cockpit door opened and he was launched from his cabin. He soared through the atmosphere of Terra. His body hit the hot sand and he looked around, not knowing where he was. No structures were in sight, only sand. He managed to pick himself up and wondered what direction to go. He felt the burning rays of the sun on his body and kept walking with his back toward the sun. He was parched and his body was getting dehydrated. He sat on the sand, exhausted, hoping someone would find him soon.

The Premier of Israel was traveling with a motorcade through the desert, exactly where Gabriel had landed. He was on his way to inspect a tunnel that the Israeli Army had built to protect all the upper governmental officials from any nuclear explosions or from possible invasion from the nearby Arab enemy. As they were nearing the entrance to the secret passageway, the bodyguards on motorbikes came to a stop. They could not believe what they were seeing and one of them pointed to a place in the ground. Gabriel heard them and stood up. He was stark naked, wearing only the gold ring. The bodyguards could not believe that there was a human being here. Gabriel started to walk towards them and all four of them pulled out their guns. They told him in Hebrew to lay down on the ground and to spread his arms and legs. Gabriel just stood there, staring at them. One soldier put his gun in the air, over his head, and fired one shot. He commanded Gabriel to lay down on the ground. Gabriel followed his orders. They handcuffed him and took him over to the motorcade. The Premier asked who he was. The soldiers replied, "He must be a spy." The Premier got out of the limousine and looked at Gabriel. He was definitely Hebrew, not Arab. The Premier asked Gabriel who he was. Gabriel replied, "I have no memory. I am lost." The Premier told the soldiers to give him a wrap and to put him in the motorcade so he could speak with him. Premier Analoff grabbed Gabriel by the chin and stared into his eyes. Gabriel stared back intensely and the Premier felt puzzled. This boy is certainly one of us, he thought, and asked the soldier standing outside the limousine to remove the handcuffs and give Gabriel his clothing. The soldier did as he was asked and handed them to Gabriel. Gabriel, never having dressed in human attire, looked at the other soldiers and proceeded to try and follow as close as he could. The trousers were right, but, when it came time for him to zip up the fly and button the waist, he was lost. The Premier watched closely, concentrating on Gabriel's movements. Gabriel pulled the zipper up and was lost when it came to the button. He left that alone and then put the jacket on. He just looked at the buttons down the front part and decided not to even try. The Premier laughed and buttoned Gabriel's jacket himself. All the soldiers could not believe their eyes. Was this really the hardcore individual that everyone said had no compassion, only love for his army? Gabriel gazed into the Premier's eyes again, only this time he felt safe. The Premier said, "Do you at least remember part of your name? "Gabriel," was the reply. The Premier took Gabriel by the hand, looked at his soldiers, and with a strong voice said, "I want to introduce you to Gabriel. He will be staying with me until we find his real origin. I want him treated with respect, and, if I find otherwise, you will be punished severely.

He then asked the soldiers to open the nearby hatch. They were astonished. They put a metal frame around the spot on the desert sand that their detector indicated. It was a lit cavern, which led to the Premier's private headquarters. They walked for about a minute when suddenly a small transporter on a track pulled up for them to ride the rest of the way. It was amazing how well concealed this tunnel was, considering it was under the desert floor.

Placing a phone call from the transmitter, Premier Analoff contacted his headquarters. He requested a meeting of the Knesset, which is a single chamber of 120 members who have the authority to vote explicitly on matters of governmental importance. When the transporter reached the destination of the headquarters, the soldiers escorted Gabriel and his trusted Premier into a hallway with an elevator. As the two entered the elevator, the doors abruptly closed, leaving behind the trained security guards. As they ascended, the Premier sensed something was wrong. The smell of smoke was very apparent. The elevator was reaching the twelfth floor when smoke encompassed the small area they were occupying. The Premier suspected sabotage. He placed his arm around Gabriel and asked him to pray with him. Gabriel asked what was happening. The Premier said they were under Arab guerilla attack and it would not be long before they would all be killed. Gabriel did not understand. He asked what was happening. The Premier said that their lives were about to end. Gabriel instinctively rubbed his gold ring. The elevator doors flew open and two armed Arab soldiers grabbed the Premier. Gabriel stepped back and told them to hand over their guns. They laughed at him and told him to lie down on the floor. Gabriel rubbed his ring again and his body started to bulge with muscle and wings. He lifted three feet from the floor and picked up both soldiers with his wings. He flew them straight up to the ceiling, crashing their skulls against the hard plaster. The soldiers were both knocked unconscious.

Gabriel lowered his body toward the Premier and laid the bodies of the Arab soldiers at his feet. Gabriel's body took on his human form again. The Premier was astonished. Was this a dream? Who is this boy? Where is he from? Perhaps he is blessed and sent here to help Israel. The Premier called an emergency code and what looked like the entire Israeli army stormed the building. They arrested the Arab soldiers and were amazed at how they had been captured. The Premier told everyone present that Gabriel was a hero and saved his life. He did not go into detail, fearing he would have to share Gabriel with all the Government.

The Premier arrived home and immediately called the Chief Justice of the Common Court. The Premier had been a widower for three years and, having no children of his own, was haunted by the loss of his family. He felt renewed love for the first time in three years and protectively wanted to adopt Gabriel.

The adoption was a private ceremony the following week. There were no questions asked as to the history of Gabriel; no one dared upset the Premier. Only the Israeli soldiers, present in the desert where Gabriel was found, knew of his unusual origin. The Premier called each soldier in, one by one, and made them take an oath of secrecy never to reveal what they witnessed. The two Arab soldiers, being tortured in the lower level prison, were the only other witnesses to the dramatic events. The Premier sent for the interrogating Israeli officers for information on the identity and nature of the Arab terrorists. The officers told him the two Arab guerillas were hallucinating about a wild man with wings who flew them up the ceiling and crashed their skulls into the plaster. They seemed to be in a kind of trance, so they administered truth serum. The only information the Arabs would reveal was of this man with wings. They must be in a severe state of shock. Fearing the Arabs would be a threat to their security and the secrecy of Gabriel, the Premier ordered that they not be interrogated again. He wanted them released to their homeland in exchange for two Israeli soldiers held in captivity.

The Premier invited all the leading dignitaries on Terra to Gabriel's bar mitzvah. David Penn, the magician, who was to perform at the dinner, was among the guests. This special event was to take place at the site of King Herod's Castle on top of a mountain, which had been converted into a synagogue.

Gabriel was being tutored for his bar mitzvah by the Rabbi who tutored the Premier forty-five years ago. For his studies, Gabriel had to learn the Torah and deliver a speech on his favorite biblical prophet. The Rabbi had never seen the likes of Gabriel. He wondered so many times during their lessons where Gabriel came from, but would not dare ask. Rabbi Segel had a white beard down to the middle of his chest, with thinning hair that he kept in a neat ponytail. His blue eyes – the color of a robin's egg – and his piercing stare were hypnotizing. He looked deeply into Gabriel's eyes for some explanation, some sign, a familiarity of nature as to where this boy belonged.

Gabriel was very aware that there was so much more of Israel to explore. He asked the Premier if he would allow him to travel about for a few hours. The request was granted. Gabriel was given a limousine from the fleet and four bodyguards. They started out early in the morning and began their tour, heading for the Red Sea. Gabriel saw the armed soldiers at the border and asked about them. He was told that the territory was divided as to who was entitled to live on the Holy Land. As they gave their passes to the soldiers, the border seemed quite friendly. Everyone waved at the passing limousine and smiled. Gabriel asked if he could see the Red Sea that he had heard about.

Gabriel watched as the glistening water grew closer and closer. As the limousine came to a halt, the smell of the water was very strong. Gabriel entertained himself on Pellisa by swimming in the Violet Sea. He told the guards to watch him from a distance, that he needed to be alone for a while. He walked quickly to the water's edge, pondering on where his brothers were and if they were safe. All of a sudden there was an image in the water next to his. He quickly turned around and could not believe his eyes. Standing next to him was a girl who had the most beautiful face he had ever seen on Terra. She spoke another language….Arabic! He asked in Hebrew, "What are you doing here?" She told him she needed to escape the stringent security of her government guards and seek some freedom on her own. She inquired about his origin. He explained he was recently adopted by Premier Analoff and that he also needed to be alone with his thoughts. She told him her father was the leader of all the Arab citizens, that they were at war with the Jews and she would never be allowed to travel here again if they knew she spoke to him. Gabriel asked what her name was. She replied, "Khadija. What is your name?" Gabriel whispered his name in her ear. She gasped. "That is the name of the angel who dictated the Koran to Muhammad; you must be a special person." They sat at the water's edge and began talking about their lives. Gabriel made arrangements to see Khadija the following day at the same place. She happily agreed.

On the home front, Premier Analoff was busy with all the preparations needed to fulfill his desire for the most astonishing bar mitzvah in all of history.

Gabriel needed to choose a story in the Old Testament to read from the lectern at the ceremony. He told the Rabbi that the story of Noah's Ark was his favorite. He was overjoyed when the rabbi agreed he could have that as his personal bar mitzvah reading.

The following day, Gabriel had the limousine take him back to the Red Sea so he could secretly meet with Khadija. As the limousine pulled into the same parking space as before, Gabriel jumped out before the driver came to a complete stop. He ran down the embankment so fast that the driver was unaware where he had gone. He saw her standing there and his heart started to beat at a rapid pace. She held out her hand and they were silent as they gazed into each other's eyes. Then Gabriel spoke, "Kahdija, I would like you to attend my bar mitzvah this weekend. You will have to disguise yourself as being of my heritage, but it would be especially pleasing to me to have you there." She told him her nanny, who raised her from an infant, often told her of the boy she truly loved but could not marry due to his being Jewish. She told Gabriel she would arrange through her nanny some disguise so she would be able to attend. It was time to go and Gabriel told her he would somehow meet with her before the bar mitzvah and have her as his special guest of honor. She was happy. She was in love. She was sure of that.

Premier Analog called the most famous magician to perform at the event. David Penn was anxious to meet the boy Gabriel Analoff. His particular curiosity was about the Premier adopting a son at a time in his life when he should be thinking about retiring and taking life easy. Why was this happening now? As David's limousine approached the Premier's estate, he was overcome with a strange sensation. When they made the final turn, which led to the main driveway, he was literally shaking.

Inside the estate, Gabriel was reading over Noah's Ark. He practiced memorizing it with as much intensity as possible. Mysteriously, his thoughts went blank, and a feeling of fear aroused in his throat and he could hardly swallow. His hands began to shake and he thought that perhaps the Arab terrorists were nearby. He put down the Torah and walked over to the window. As David approached the front door, he felt that a force as strong as the one at Jude Moroni's home was also here at Premier Analoff's home. David proceeded to ring the bell and was escorted into the library.

Gabriel had heard about David Penn and was thrilled that he was going to perform a magical trick at his bar mitzvah party. Gabriel entered the library cautiously, still feeling a strong vibration of fear. David Penn felt the force before he turned around and faced Gabriel. David stood up from the sofa and extended his hand. Gabriel reached out and shook his hand, never leaving eye contact. They both just stared at one another. Finally, David asked if he were Gabriel. Gabriel acknowledged David with a friendly smile and asked if he could get him a drink. Gabriel summoned the butler, who brought David a drink – scotch and water. He announced that the Premier would be detained for two hours. David offered Gabriel a drive around the city to look at some of the ancient ruins. He agreed.

As they drove down dirt roads, they were filled with a sense of wonder as to the history behind this great country of Israel. They pulled over and sat under a tree near the road and, before they could have any conversation, a small Arab boy put out his hand in friendship for them to shake. They did not know where he came from. David watched as Gabriel shook the hand of this Arab boy. When the boy reached out for David's hand, it was a whole different story. David stepped back and yelled to the boy in Hebrew to leave them alone. The Arab boy ran down the hill and was out of sight in no time. When they got into the car, it did not start. David told Gabriel to stay in the car and that he would go down to the town to get help. No sooner had David left the car when the same boy walked up and looked into the car window at Gabriel. He started yelling, "You are a Jew and you do not deserve to be here!" Gabriel watched as ten more boys gathered around the car and started rocking it back and forth. Gabriel rubbed his gold ring and all of a sudden the windows blew out of the car. The hood started detaching from the window guards and all the boys were knocked down from the force. Gabriel jumped out and began feeling different. His body was expanding again and his wings took the place of his arms. He started to fly around ten feet above them, hovering over like an eagle in flight. The boys panicked. Unable to move, Gabriel landed in the midst of them and told all of them to stand up. They did so slowly, each one more frightened than the other. One by one, Gabriel told them to approach him. He asked each one why they wanted to harm him. "Because Jews are bad." Gabrlel then asked if they thought harming him would help the Arabs to obtain their wish and goals. Gabriel explained that by loving your brothers as yourself you can obtain peace on Terra and stop the horrible war. They said the Jews were to blame for the bloodshed. Gabriel asked them which one would have killed him. They all stood in silence. He asked them to examine their conscience and if he did anything wrong to justify his murder. No one uttered a word. Gabriel told them he would change their lives today and he would invite them to his bar mitzvah party. They could not believe their ears. He then made each one tell him in their own language what they wanted for the future of Israel. All of them said peace. He told them to pray for it and that them starting to find peace in their own hearts was a beginning. They watched in awe while Gabriel transformed back to his human form. Gabriel told them it was a trick he learned when he was young and he would never reveal it to anyone. They just looked at him in amazement. David Penn pulled up with a tow truck and mechanic to fix his car. When he saw the car, he thought a bomb attack took place. Gabriel told David it was a miracle he was not harmed.

The morning of the bar mitzvah, Gabriel asked if he could drive down to the water for some meditation time alone. The chauffeur drove Gabriel down to the Red Sea and parked in his usual spot, which was far enough away so that Gabriel could meditate alone. He ran all the way thinking Khadija would be there waiting for him. She was not there. He assumed she would arrive any time now. She did not show up. He waited one hour, which seemed a lifetime. Where was she? Did her father find out about their meeting? He felt a knot in his stomach and a faintness in his head. What was happening to him? What kind of an effect was Khadija having on him? Was this a normal human emotion?

The chauffeur beeped the horn and Gabriel walked ever so slowly to the car, hoping the detainment would bring him a glimpse of his beloved.

David Penn was preparing for his new trick to be performed in front of many world diplomats and world leaders at Gabriel's bar mitzvah. He looked over his wardrobe, which consisted mostly of the colors black and white. These colors give an almost magical effect to a dark and smoke-filled stage. David was nervous. Where did Gabriel find the strength to hoard off those attackers on the road? Where did Premier Analoff find this God-send? He was determined to get these answers today.

Gabriel was dressed in a pinstripe vested suit. He looked handsome. He approached the Premier in his bedroom just before they left for the temple. Extending his hand in a friendly gesture, Gabriel expressed his sincere appreciation and gratitude for all the Premier had done for him. The Premier hugged Gabriel and told him that, from this day forward, he would call him son and he was to call him father. This was a very intense moment for Premier Analoff. He felt for the first time in his life that this boy was truly a part of him. His love for his wife remained strong, but not like this. This was like his own soul was standing next to him.

It was time for the limousine drive to the temple, where at the top of the mountain the old palace of King Herod remained as it did 2000 years ago, only restored in a modern way to accommodate bar mitzvahs.

As they approached the temple, there were hundreds of security guards checking all limousines as they passed through the gate. Security was tight. Gabriel was so excited. He knew the story of the Bible and how the Creator saved the Israelites from enslavement. He looked forward to the reading of Noah's Ark. He knew he would feel the presence of the Creator, the way he did on Pellisa. He was so looking forward to that peaceful feeling when the Creator's Spirit would be circling around him again.

The huge double doors to the palace were wide open and all of the invited guests were seated in a large, domed room. The altar was brightly lit with glowing candles. The podium was made of marble and, as the Rabbi and Gabriel approached it, the guests drew silent. Rabbi Segel introduced himself and then Gabriel. He looked out at the crowd and could not believe all he recognized. The President of the United States was seated in the front row with the Emperor of Japan. The Rabbi spoke of the love Gabriel had shown to all since his arrival and how he would work towards ending the war not only in Israel but around the world with his Universal Youth Core.

Gabriel started reading the Torah and everyone was mesmerized. He spoke passionately of Noah and referred to him as his brother. All were in awe. In telling the part where Noah brought on the ark two animals of every species, Gabriel compared this to how Terra could be saved as with Noah's Ark, if two humans male and female, of each nationality started their own countries, without prejudice amongst them. He reminded them of the dove that Noah sent out several times that finally came back with a twig, meaning it found dry land. He stated that the twig is like the word of the

Creator—if there is solid faith and belief in the Creator, His word will never fail you. His love is greater than the Universe. He is our Father and will supply all our needs if we only ask. Everyone was in total amazement that this newly adopted son of the Premier's was so spiritually connected. They loved hearing him speak and they felt a true peace listening to him.

The main dining hall was set up like a supper club, with a stage at the center and a circular red spotlight lighting the spot where David was to perform his magical trick.

With everyone seated for dinner, Premier Analoff offered a toast to all that were there to witness this very special event. He asked that they bow their heads in prayer and asked the Creator to bless Gabriel and all present.

After dinner, a red spotlight on the stage went off. Everyone sat in complete darkness for one minute. All of a sudden, the spotlight was on the doorway where David Penn flew onto the stage. Everyone stood and cheered. David looked extraordinary in his white turtleneck sweater and black baggy pants, and his eyes were so emerald green that they looked surreal.

David was just about to call Gabriel to the stage when he saw a female figure standing in the back of the room. She was the most beautiful woman he had ever seen. Her black hair was to her waist and she wore a black cocktail dress that made her figure look like an hourglass. David grabbed the red spotlight and put it on her. She gasped in horror. He asked if anyone in the audience could identify this gorgeous creature. Khadija could not speak. Gabriel jumped to his feet and ran to her. He placed his arm around her. David Penn requested Gabriel bring the beautiful one up to the stage with him. He took her hand as they approached the stage and both were trembling. David asked Gabriel if this was his girlfriend. Gabriel replied, "She is my future wife." Premier Analoff was astounded. He could see the girl looked Arab. This could not be happening. Maybe she just had the dark features and was really Hebrew. David asked her name. Everyone watched as David turned Khadija around on her heels and stared into her gorgeous black eyes. He placed his hands on her shoulders and asked when the wedding was to take place. She said it was yet to be planned but probably in the very near future. She looked at Gabriel and he took her hand. David studied Khadija from head to toe. She wore a Star of David necklace, which baffled him. She did not look Jewish. He would use his expertise to investigate. David asked Khadija to close her eyes tightly. She still held on to Gabriel's hand. She felt a sense of fear as David asked her to explain the meaning of the bar mitzvah. She felt her throat starting to close and began to tremble. Gabriel felt her hand quivering and asked David to stop. David continued; Khadija opened her eyes. She looked at the audience with a sincere glance and began to speak. "The meaning of the word bar mitzvah is that, when a Jewish boy or girl reaches the age of 13, they assume the moral and religious duties of an adult. Loyalty to the Creator, family and all humanity in general is specified, especially treating others as you would like to be treated." The room became dark and the spotlight was shining on her when David asked when her bat mitzvah was. She held onto her Star of David necklace. David asked her to close her eyes. She immediately went into a trance. David then asked her to tell him what she was thinking. Khadija said she was on a carousel and her father was holding her hand. She wanted to reach out for the gold ring but she was too small to reach it. Her father reached out and grabbed it for her and told her to make a wish. She remembers wishing that the day would never end, as her rare times spent with her father was her happiest of times. She said all his advisors and his army were what took up most of his time. David then asked her who her father was. Gabriel, wishing to protect Khadija, said she was his special guest and that David should stop interrogating her. David kept up his flow of questions and Khadija told the audience her father was the Premier of all the Arab states. Everyone gasped. Premier Analoff stood up and walked onto the stage. He took her hand and she opened her eyes. "My child," he said, "why are you here?" She replied, "I love Gabriel." All the crowd gasped. David removed the spell from her and she had no idea what had just transpired.

Premier Analoff took both Gabriel and Khadija aside. He wanted to know what was going on. They both told him they were in love. He asked them to just take their time and said that all would work out for them. Premier Analoff could not believe that he finally found his dream child and now an Arab girl would be taking him away. He knew the power of first love and that he should prepare himself to give Gabriel the freedom to think he was in control of the situation.

David the magician was now in an uproar inside. His magical trick was not going to have the same effect since the announcement of Khadija and Gabriel's promise of marriage. He asked the audience to stand up. They did so and he asked if any one of them could fly. They all looked at one another and laughed. David then asked all of them to place their hands on their shoulders. David then put the spotlight on the audience. All of them started to ascend to the ceiling. He then flew up there himself and told the people to flap their arms up and down and to follow him. He flew around the perimeter of the walls in the huge domed room and then proceeded to fly out the door, motioning for them to follow. Premier Analoff and Gabriel were astounded. When David flew out of the front door of the castle, all followed in single file. David flew around the top of the palace with all the dignitaries following him. It was the most astounding sight anyone had ever seen. The security force outside just watched in sheer amazement while David flew Premier Analoff's guests around the top of the mountain. When they were at the highest peak, David lowered himself to land. They all followed. He asked them if they were okay. They were all so thrilled to be able to fly and they started to ask him if they would be able to have this spell kept on them forever. David said it was only a trick and it would be off the minute they returned to the palace.

The palace was now buzzing with reporters from all the surrounding area and television cameras trying to get footage of the flying diplomats. When they finally were flying back to the palace, the limousine approaching the palace was that of Judge Moroni and his son Michael, who was invited to mix with the diplomats of the foreign countries and also to speak to Gabriel about forming the Universal Youth Core. When they saw the flock of humans descending upon the palace, they pulled over and got out of the limousine and watched as they landed. Michael looked at his father and told him that David Penn was near. Judge Moroni then remembered that the Premier stated on the invitation that there would be entertainment, and he thought it odd that there would be a show at such a holy event. Then he looked at Michael. They both knew David was here.

The door leading to the palace was still heavily guarded. Judge Moroni showed his identification and they entered the grounds. When they started entering the palace, Michael felt his heart pounding. How could this be? David was in the reception area having a drink when he felt the force. He knew Michael was here.

Gabriel was led by Premier Analoff to be introduced to Michael and Judge Moroni. Michael put his hand out to shake Gabriel's and they both felt the force of their true being. Michael asked Gabriel if they could speak alone. They walked out onto the grounds and Michael said, "Hello my brother, Gabriel." They embraced and Michael told Gabriel of the evil that was present in the palace and that David would try to destroy their mission. Gabriel listened in awe.

Michael and Gabriel approached the room where David sat. They entered together and walked up to the famous magician. They both took one of his hands and led him out to the grounds.

David trembled; he knew this was a strength not human. He

looked hard into their eyes and knew they were both of the same origin. Where? How? Why are they here on Terra? David had heard conversation of the Universal Youth Core and believed Michael was in charge. Now he was getting the picture loud and clear. They both were trying to bring brotherhood to this planet. Both Michael and Gabriel looked at David and simultaneously rubbed their gold rings. David turned into the horrifying satanic form. He lifted off the ground and it was then that Michael and Gabriel told him their power was of the Creator and that it was much greater than his own. David knew he could not break through this strength—for it was from the greatest force in the Universe. David transformed back to his human form and they all stared at one another. David knew he was defeated. He would go to another country to be free to destroy the human spirit. He had the driver take him to his hotel, where he packed, called the airlines and booked a flight to Russia. There were a lot of Bosnia countries in chaos and the temptation he would bring there would be worth the trip.

Michael and Gabriel sat in the garden and talked of arranging a meeting with the United Nations Youth to get an organization formed that would surpass any other on Terra for world peace.

Premier Analoff went out to the gardens and summoned Gabriel to come back to his party and to mingle with his guests who had traveled from all parts of Terra to honor him. Michael and Gabriel went back to the palace, both feeling much better after having found each other, and they hoped to locate their other four brothers in the near future. They desperately needed to warn them of the danger of David Penn.

Raphael
RUSSIA

Chapter Three

RAPHAEL

*R*aphael's landing looked like it was going very smoothly. He was heading towards a thick forest and his rocket was flashing bright colored lights, beaming in for an open space to land among the trees. In the center of this vast forest was a castle.

As the rocket hovered over the treetops, the ship chamber carrying Raphael opened and he landed on the right side of the castle. The Premier of Russia lived there with his sixteen year old daughter Katrina. He kept their home as if it were the 17th century. Katrina had blue-black hair to her waist, piercing violet eyes and beautiful milk-white skin. Her beauty was so rare that a painting could never capture the quality of her loveliness, inside and outside.

Katrina watched the stars appear in the dusk from her bedroom window. She noticed flickering lights – assembled next to each other and shaped like a giant star – approaching closer and closer. She got up from her bed and sat on the windowsill. As the lights became larger and closer, her heart started pounding faster and faster. Katrina knew someone had landed on the grounds and pondered on the idea of summoning the guards to search the property. Then a strange feeling came over her. She remembered her tutor speaking of the Greek Gods from long ago who had wondrous powers, and some of them could fly. Could this possibly be one of them returning to Terra after so many centuries? Katrina immediately put the light out in her room so the servants would believe she was asleep, for she intended to see for herself who or what was out there. She was not afraid.

Katrina put on her warmest clothing and set out to find the enchanted being. She cautiously walked down the hallway until she came to the hidden staircase that led to the wine cellar. This was next to the servants' quarters, which Katrina believed was near where the unknown had landed. She slowly made her way towards the trap doors. She picked up the keys on the wall, which would open both the steel doors and the main door to the wine cellar. She knew her father forbade her to go outside after dusk and that she would be severely punished if he found out.

She loved her father deeply; only his possessiveness was quite stifling. After her mother's death, she had been kept almost a prisoner in this palace she called home. The world she knew consisted of the inside walls and the gardens around the castle. She had a tutor give her the proper schooling since her father refused to have her exposed to the outside world. He saw his wife, who he loved almost insanely, in his Katrina. No one was going to influence her to leave him. If she were to marry, he would fix the nuptials to his liking and they would live with him. His Katrina would live under his roof as long as he was alive.

She descended to the lower level, and, as she made her way toward the steel doors, she heard footsteps. She crawled under a table and stared at a huge cobweb on one of the table's legs as she held her breath. The cellar became brighter as she heard a voice yell, "Who goes there?" Katrina froze. She knew the voice so well. It was her father's driver. He would not let her go outside if he found her, so she kept silent. She snuggled closer to the wall so her skirt would not show from under the table. She held her many layers of undergarments with both hands. The footsteps grew closer and she stopped breathing altogether. Seeing nothing, the cellar became dark again.

She placed the key in the hole of the steel doors and pushed her shoulders upwards until the doors opened to the gardens. Katrina smelled the fresh air outdoors and breathed it in again and again to her lungs. She crawled onto the lawn, inching her way close to the stone wall structure. She noticed movement near a snowdrift. She thought at first it was a deer, but, as she focused on the moving object, she saw a human form. He appeared to be glowing. It was his naked body reflecting rays from the moon. She thought to herself that this must be a Greek God from time past. The ancient history course her tutor taught her last year about the Greek Gods and Goddesses must have really existed. She moved in closer to him and, trembling, she spoke, "You came from the sky, who are you?" She looked so shocked by his nakedness. Raphael did not know that this lovely creature who stood before him was the 17 year old Katrina, the daughter of the Premier of Russia. When she asked if he was a Greek God, Raphael replied, "You and I have the same Creator. The Creator of the Universe. He made the creatures large and small. He made all things. He loves us above all else." Katrina listened in awe as Raphael spoke more and more about the Creator.

She informed Raphael that her father would soon be looking for her and that they must make up a story so he could stay at their castle long enough for him to accomplish on Terra what the Creator hoped for. She told him that his Terra mission would be her life's ambition from this moment on. Katrina suggested that they tell her father the truth. Raphael agreed and they proceeded to the castle, with Katria putting her leather apron around Raphael's naked body.

Raphael took Katrina's hand and asked her to pray with him for her father's acceptance. They both knelt in the snow and Raphael prayed, "Dear Creator, you have made Heaven and Terra and all planets. You are the Creator of our wonderful Universe. Please open the Premier's heart and mind to comprehend my mission. Please make him a believer in You. Let not my will be done but Yours. Amen."

As they approached the entrance to the wine cellar, Katrina panicked. The wine cellar doors were closed tightly. The housekeeper must have felt the draft upstairs and decided to investigate. How would they enter without her father knowing she was outside? Neither one of them had a coat on. Katrina went to the servant's quarters and told Raphael to wait for her. She thought she would get him some clothing. She went into the small bungalow and in the closet was a long, very large raccoon coat. She grabbed it and ran out before being seen. She placed it on Raphael. The barn was next door so they made their way there for shelter. The hay was stacked 20 feet high, and, while both of them shivered, Katrina felt warm and safe here in Raphael's arms as he held her close to him. She was feeling a bit light-headed and only wanted him to hold her for the rest of her life. She felt so content. Katrina wanted these precious moments to never end.

They approached the large doors of the castle slowly and with much caution. A servant, seeing Katrina, opened the door and they both entered. Katrina's father was still sleeping so she told Raphael to stay in the study on the sofa until her father woke up. She went upstairs and told the butler to take care of Raphael's needs. Katrina lay on her bed, dreaming of her recent adventure. She thought of what she would tell her father. She wanted Raphael to stay. She hoped that the prayer they said together would be answered.

The Premier had a difficult night sleeping. He kept having nightmares that Katrina was in danger. He awoke in a sweat and felt he needed to check on her immediately. He ran down the lengthy hallway and, instead of knocking on her door, as he always allowed her privacy, he burst into her bedroom. Katrina was lying there, daydreaming about Raphael. The Premier said, "Are you alright, Katrina?" She replied, "Oh Father, I am so happy." He ran to her and put his arms around her, almost smothering her. He replied, "I was so afraid you were hurt. I had bad dreams Katrina, and I want you to be safe here forever. You are my only hope for happiness. Without you my life would not be worth living." "Oh, father, I am fine, and I can't wait to tell you." And when she paused, he looked into her eyes and said, "Katrina, tell me why you are beaming and happiness flows from you." Katrina said, "Father, I love you very much. You have provided a home and love for me all my life; I want for nothing, not until last night." Her father replied, "Anything you wish will be granted, name it." Katrina looked directly into his loving eyes and said, "Father, when I reveal this to you, please....understand. I was watching my hawks fly into their usual patterns last night when suddenly I saw a flash of light. I followed it out to the gardens. A spaceship with multi-colored lights hovered over the grounds." He interrupted, "It is the Americans, they are spying on us. I'll kill all of them."

He immediately proceeded to call the Kremlin and make arrangements for a full investigation of the incident and to complete a search of the grounds. He was quickly on the road to Moscow to meet with top government heads of state. Katrina ran to the study and told Raphael what happened. He told her they needed to contact the American Embassy and warn them of a threat of nuclear war. Raphael told Katrina that once they reached the Ambassador of the United States they could explain that it was his rocket from Pellisa that the Premier is referring to and that he was here on a mission of peace.

Katrina contacted the American Embassy in Moscow. She gave the phone to Raphael. He told the Ambassador he was a friend to all the countries of Terra and he was here on a peace mission from another galaxy. One of his brothers was in the United States of America and, if he did not act quickly, the Premier would be sending over the KGB to arrest him, and he would not be released until they found the spaceship Katrina witnessed. "It is now circling Terra waiting for my return to the planet Pellisa. Please trust and verify my message."

The United States Ambassador was extremely confused. Was this a trick to make him call the White House and would the KGB tape the conversation and accuse him of spying? He secretly coded the message so it could never be interpreted by any known code system in Moscow. Within fifteen minutes, the President of the United States summoned Judge Moroni to the Oval Office. The President asked his friend and colleague if it could be related to the Universal Youth Core. Judge Jude reinforced the truth by summoning Michael to the White House. Michael stood in front of the President of the United States and replied, "Mr. President, we have come to this planet from 400 billion light years away. My galaxy is called Tau Ceti, and our planet's name is Pellisa. Yes, one of my brothers was sent to Russia, but I have yet to hear from him. Our species have never seen death or evil. We walk our gardens with the Creator and live in peace and harmony, the way Terra was intended until it fell into sin. The mission my five brothers and I are here to accomplish is to bring the planet Terra into one family. All of Terra will be destroyed by nuclear warheads if they do not repent and show to our universal brothers all can be fed, clothed and cared for by one heavenly Father who made them all." The President immediately sent a secret coded message to the Ambassador in Moscow. It told him to give complete confidence to Raphael. The Ambassador was relieved a bit, since the importance of all secret coded messages and information would be someone else's responsibility. The KGB, moments later, broke into the room and insisted the Ambassador lie on the floor. They blindfolded him, put him on a stretcher and carried him off to be interrogated. All his colleagues wondered what had happened and the Kremlin decided to tell them he had heart failure. If they wanted to speak with him, they would be notified when he was able to receive company.

Raphael and Katrina sat in the study and rehearsed what they would tell her father, the Premier. Katrina asked: if the Creator was all good, why did he permit suffering on Terra? Raphael proceeded to tell her of Lucifer and how he tempts the people of Terra. Eliminating the Creator from their lives and making government their idol was what Satan wanted. He did not have to tempt as much, for some lived only for worldly causes, spiritually empty of the true meaning of life. Government power was taught to them to be of most importance, and this alone was bound to doom their country of Russia and all of the communist countries. Katrina listened and believed him. When they heard the huge front door open and the Premier ordering the butler to summon Katrina, they both froze. The Premier went into the kitchen for some brandy when Katrina approached him. Smiling, she said, "Father, there is something I must tell you, but before I do, please hear all that I have to tell you." The Premier looked kindly and told his daughter to speak her mind. "What I have told you of the lights falling from the sky and the spaceship is true. This creature from another planet is made to look like us, and his mission is to bring peace to Terra. His five brothers are now living in the United States, Israel, China, Palestine and Spain. You are picked by the Creator of our Universe to house Raphael, one of the sextuplets from Pellisa, which is light years from our Terra. His Creator is our Creator; we are all created equal by the same living spirit. He made all the Universe. Please have an open mind and do not think him to be a spy from the United States. His love of all humanity is real. Father, if you will accept him, you will be helping our Russian country to develop as a world family. Take him and interrogate him privately. He will show you signs that will convince you. His knowledge is above any intelligence on our planet. I love him father, and as your daughter I ask only that you trust him and grow to love him as I do." The Premier replied, "Bring him to me, Katrina."

Raphael trembled. He prayed silently to the Creator to open up the eyes of this man who only knew the Kremlin as his God and let some light open his mind to another advanced power. The Premier looked into Raphael's eyes and said, "Where do you call home, son?" Raphael answered, "It is Pellisa, the most beautiful and advanced of all planets. We walk the gardens with the Creator of all the Universe. He loves you and Katrina and myself the same as he loves His angels. The Premier replied, "How do I know this to be true?" Raphael told the Premier to put his head back on the chair rest and to relax and close his eyes. Hesitating, the Premier complied with Raphael's wishes. Raphael prayed aloud holding his gold ring, "Dear Creator, please give him a vision of proof so he will believe." The Premier started visioning the halls of the Kremlin. The leaders of all the nations were walking toward him. All of a sudden, there appeared a crystal ball in the center between them, which was resting on a tripod. A voice told them to look into the possible future of Terra. The heads of all the countries glanced down at the crystal ball and saw Terra rotating on its axis and then the globe became smaller and smaller and the stars appeared. From the territory of Russia came three nuclear rockets heading toward the United States. The United States territory then launched off seven rockets, all aimed at main cities in Russia. Then out of Russia came 22 rockets that were going astray. All the remaining countries launched rockets to their so-called enemies. It seems every country but Israel was in ruins. The entire Terra was being destroyed by the fire of nuclear power and the explosions were so fierce and loud that the United States President embraced the Russian Premier. They began sobbing and the other heads of all the countries were holding their eyes with their hands, not able to watch any more destruction. The Premier awoke from the vision and stared at Raphael. He said to him, "I will do all I can to save Terra. Whatever you wish,

Raphael, will be granted." Katrina walked into the room and saw the Russian Premier hugging Raphael. She was ecstatic. The Premier told Katrina, "Behold your new brother, whom I will adopt."

The Premier immediately called for a celebration. He told his staff to prepare for a major event of adoption at the Palace in Moscow and to invite all the Heads of State throughout Terra. He said they must prepare a party and to invite the very best entertainment. They immediately called David Penn, the most renowned magician.

Jophiel

PALESTINE

Chapter Four

JOPHIEL

The six-pointed spacecraft headed for Palestine. The fourth penguin felt his body changing at a rapid pace. He felt and watched his fur falling off, and his body was becoming chilled. He knew this was part of the Creator's plan, yet he could not understand why he was losing all his fur. He reached down to feel his webbed feet only to feel the small-boned, skin-covered human feet of the being he was headed toward. He reached for his head only to feel the foreign form of something he could not imagine. He held onto his golden ring very tightly. The hatch door of his space unit opened and he was launched through the sky. As he was approaching Palestine, Jophiel saw a large building for which he was headed.

This building was called a Mosque and it was where all the Muslims were worshipping Allah. It was crowded, with thousands of religious devoted believers chanting. They could be heard clearer and clearer as Jophiel felt the vibration of gravity pulling him into the atmosphere of Terra. He watched the Mosque appearing closer and closer and suddenly he closed his eyes as the impact hit. He landed next to the back door of the building. Opening his eyes, he saw women in black dresses and black veils walking outside the Mosque. Men were on their knees inside the building, striking their hearts with their hands and chanting Arabic praises to Allah.

Children watched as Jophiel landed and they began screaming, "There is a naked boy lying on the ground." The women rushed over to where Jophiel lay. He looked into the eyes of one elderly woman whose facial veil covered all of her face except for her eyes. She looked at him, cautiously at first. Then she picked up his head with her hands and whispered gently in Arabic in his ear, "Who are you?" Jophiel replied, "I am Jophiel. I do not know where I am." The woman's heart went out to him, and she immediately called for a blanket to cover his nakedness.

The boys who discovered Jophiel ran into the Mosque screaming, "There is a naked stranger outside, perhaps he is an Israeli terrorist." The entire congregation stood up and began to flood out of the Mosque. Surrounding Jophiel, the crowds, some pointing their fingers at him, yelled in Arabic, "Arrest him, he is an Israeli terrorist." The Premier of the government in Palestine, as well as the heads of three other Arab territories, were curious as to the commotion going on outside the Mosque. They also pushed their way to where Jophiel lay, followed by their security guards circling these high officials to protect them from any possible attack. Jophiel put his arm out and said in Arabic, "I am hurting, is there anyone here who can help me?"

Premier Abdul Arrat, the leader of the Palestine government, told his bodyguards to carry this boy into the Mosque, where they laid him on the floor of the back room. Premier Arrat asked that the leaders of the three other countries remain with him in the room and for all the others to leave. The Premier then took off his long headdress and tied it around Jophiel's waist. When Jophiel was made comfortable, they all sat around a table and began questioning him.

They asked Jophiel his name and if he was a Muslim. When

Jophiel told them his name in Arabic, they remembered an angel of long ago that had the same name. On hearing this, they asked him if he knew and could recite any words from the Koran. Jophiel closed his eyes and held on tightly to his gold ring. He said in perfect Arabic, "In all of Arab history, Muhammad brought the word of the Creator to your people so you could be blessed with peace. Instead, you still bring terror to your fellow man and do not follow the working miracle the Creator brought to you through Muhammad. You must follow the Koran entirely and not bring war to any of your Terra brothers. I am here on a mission of peace. My brothers and I are to stop a nuclear war and help you understand that all are created equal and live under one Creator. I know Him and He is the one you are to worship. There is only one Creator of all. You must love your neighbor as yourself."

Premier Arrat was shocked and asked all the other Muslim leaders to step out of the room. He then held Jophiel's hand and asked him what he could do to help him on his mission. Jophiel replied, "Let me start a universal club for all the youth on Terra, teaching all can live together as one family."

Premier Arrat called for his limousine to bring him and Jophiel back to his residence. He told Jophiel he was going to stay with him at his home. He told the other Arab leaders Jophiel was truly Arab and that he was to personally take care of him.

When their limousine pulled up outside the Premier's mansion, security surrounded the automobile while they were escorted into the home. Jophiel felt very tense with the events happening, so he asked Premier Arrat if he could have some place to rest alone. He was brought into a guest room where he immediately fell into a deep sleep on this luxurious bed.

Premier Arrat summoned his wife, Medina. It was only a year since their only son, Mohammed, had been killed by Israei soldiers —he was flying a helicopter over territory forbidden by the Israeli government and was shot down. Premier Arrat began doubting not only the Creator, but why this could happen to Mohammad. He was not on a military mission. He just went off course and, without any warning, was shot down. His son was not carrying spy photography equipment or a bomb. The only son of this extremely popular political figure was merely testing his new helicopter for technical purposes. He was a peacemaker and felt killing innocent children with terrorist attacks was against anything he believed in. His mission was to make peace with Israel. When Mohammad Arrat lost his life at the hands of the Jews, Premier Arrat lost all faith in any kind of peace in the future while he was still Premier.

Medina Arrat walked into the library of her husband. She still wore black in mourning her son's death. She wore a black veil over her swollen eyes all the time. The veil hid her almost closed eyes that were never free from tears. Her heart was heavy with grief over her only son Mohammed's death. Premier Arrat spoke to Medina and began telling her about Jophiel. He asked her help in providing a warm welcome to this stranger. She did not understand why this boy was brought here, but she agreed to go into the guest room and greet him.

As Medina entered Jophiel's room, she was shocked to see him sound asleep and lying across the bed, with only her husband's headdress tied around his waist. She quietly walked across the room and sat next to him on the bed. She looked at his face and she began to feel a rush of motherly love. Was this truly a gift from Allah? The face of Jophiel was astonishingly handsome and his features were so truly Muslim. He was the same age as her son and Medina leaned over him to stroke his forehead. Jophiel awakened and looked into Medina's eyes. He immediately felt her warmth. She told him to rest and that she would have some broth and tea prepared for him. She prayed in silence and thanked Allah for this gift of love. She would see that he was protected from harm. The following day she made arrangements for Jophiel to have all her son Mohammed's clothing. She gave him her son's bedroom and then entered her daughter Khadija's bedroom to joyfully announce she now had a brother again.

News spread quickly around all of the Arab territories that Premier Arrat was making plans to adopt Jophiel as a son and that he would probably be groomed as the heir to the Premier.

Every day Jophiel studied the Koran, and soon he started to accompany Premier Arrat to political rallies. He was welcomed to join with the Arab commonwealth, of which he was beginning to become the center. He gave speeches of love and worldly brotherhood. His reputation spread and people began to flock from every part of Palestine to see the man who spoke of every human as being equal under one Creator. He was starting to awaken in the citizens a spirit of cooperation unknown in their recent terrorist history.

Jophiel overheard Medina preparing for the celebration of his adoption as their son. She made plans to invite heads of state from all around Terra. Jophiel felt so loved and wanted. He walked in to ask her if he could speak with her privately. He told her how much he loved her and appreciated all that she was doing to make this a memorable occasion. She just hugged him and told him it was her wish. She asked him to make a list of everyone he wanted to attend.

The next evening, Jophiel could not sleep. He went into the library and picked up the Koran. He knew every word by heart. He sat by the fireplace and began meditating on this sacred book. He was saddened by how much strife there was between his country and Israel and all the terrorism being committed by his people who formed the terrorist factions. How could humans place bombs on themselves and drive into marketplaces just to kill some Jewish citizens? It made absolutely no sense. He went upstairs to dress to go out. Instead, he went to the servants' quarters and knocked on the door. The butler answered and Jophiel asked if he could borrow his Jeep. The Jeep was around ten years old and Jophiel felt he could mingle with his people better if they did not know his identity. He drove the Jeep and stopped when he reached the Gaza strip. He parked and started walking around the area. There were soldiers with guns surrounding most of the area. He walked into a nearby café and sat down. The owner asked him what he wanted to drink. Jophiel asked for a cup of coffee. The owner brought it to him and then asked where he was from. Jophiel said he was not from the area and soon sensed the owner was unfriendly, as he had gone into the office and called someone over to investigate Jophiel. He thought, since Jophiel was so secretive about his residence, perhaps he was a spy. Jophiel paid for his coffee and quickly went into the jeep and headed even further into the dangerous territory.

Jophiel saw a set of high beam lights coming toward him. He flashed his lights so as to warn the driver to lower his. He could not see anything, being blinded by the bright light. He came to a complete stop when he realized he was completely surrounded by Israeli soldiers with guns pointing directly at him. He slowly got out of the Jeep. They took his keys and opened the back hatch. They removed a rug and underneath were rifles and grenades. Jophiel panicked. Why would his butler not tell him what was in the Jeep? Then Jophiel realized his butler must belong to a terrorist group.

The soldiers put Jophiel in the back of an Army truck, handcuffed him and transported him to their headquarters for interrogation in Jerusalem.

The Israeli soldiers placed Jophiel in a room which had a large movie screen. They told him to watch the film closely. There on the screen was Premier Arrat surrounded by PLO police, who were outside a Mosque affiliated with Islamic militants in the Gaza strip. The printing on the screen stated it was the beginning of a civil war. The news declared Premier Arrat has great military power but bullets alone could not sustain his government. He must remember that most of his police have relatives. It is for sure that they will think twice before shooting their own people. The blood feud with themselves cannot be settled until the Islamic militants unleash suicide bomb attacks on Israeli targets. Jophiel was in shock. Could this be propaganda or was this film he was watching truly the belief of his people? The Israeli police still did not know the true identity of the handcuffed prisoner.

Jophiel looked at the Jewish soldiers and asked them why they were holding him. They replied that he was an Arab and as such was considered a potential terrorist. Having weapons under a rug in his Jeep was not a good sign. Then Jophiel told them who he was and they were in disbelief. Could this be possible? The son of the most important political Arab was sitting right in front of them. Then Jophiel told the soldiers that Gabriel, the Premier's newly adopted son, was known to him. Jophiel told them to call Gabriel at the Palace. They would know he spoke the truth and that he and Gabriel were working together for all the good of Israel and the whole of Terra. They called the Palace and kept Jophiel highly guarded.

Jophiel walked over to the barred window and looked out. He saw Jerusalem's first light dancing on the ancient stone as the sun rose from behind the desert mountains across the Jordan and the Dead Sea, and rays touched the curve of the Mount of Olives. This city, Jophiel thought, has narrow alleys and secluded courtyards where small communities of Jews, Muslims, Armenians, Greek Orthodox, Roman Catholics and other ethnic and religious groups resided with intense devotion to their traditions and their faiths. He could hear the calls and chants in the eerie half light of the Old City mingle in an overlapping minor key like separate strains of the same plaintive melody. All the pious in Jerusalem who greet the dawn—the Muslims, Jews and Christians sacrifice sleep for early morning prayers. Shadows move among the narrow twisting alleyways, Orthodox Jews in broad brimmed black hats, long black coats, black trousers and full beards walk quietly to and from the wall, passing Arabs who wear white kerchiefs, draped gracefully over their heads and held by circular thongs. The eyes of the Jews and of the Arabs slide past each other. Perhaps one gives a slight, silent nod to the other as they pass in the final moments of the night. Jophiel wondered if, in the future, Jews and Arabs would live side by side with their spiritual hearts, offering thanksgiving to the one Creator who loved them all.

The jail door opened and Gabriel was standing in the doorway. He began to cry tears of joy upon the sight of Jophiel. Gabriel exclaimed, "My brother, you are alive!" The Jewish soldiers were silent in disbelief. How could a Jewish leader's son and an Arab leader's son be brothers?

Jophiel watched the faces of the Jewish soldiers as they observed the joyous reunion of Jophiel and his brother Gabriel. With Gabriel was his father, Premier Analoff. Then he asked for the soldiers' attention. Gabriel began to speak. "This is my brother Jophiel. He and I are from another solar system in the Universe and we were sent here to make peace on Terra by the Creator, who is the Father of the Universe. It is up to our governments to stop wars and bring peace and love to all the land. We must start by heeding the words of our Creator to love one another as we love ourselves. Jophiel and I and our four other brothers were sent here to live among you in many countries to bring an end to destruction and hate. Our planet, Pellisa, has no death or evil. We walk the gardens with the Creator and trust and love Him, as should you. Hopefully, in time, we will succeed in our mission to bring to Terra peace and hope." With those words, the Premier and Gabriel and Jophiel left the prison to head back to the Army headquarters.

Premier Analoff called Premier Arrat. Premier Arrat was so overwhelmed with joy to learn Jophiel was safe. Jophiel spoke to his father and proceeded to tell him the full story. Premier Analoff listened, absolutely amazed by the talk of the power of the Creator. He also spoke to Premier Arrat to say he would be privileged to meet with him privately for negotiations to prepare a peace agreement far more effective than the previous ones that seemed to only cause more friction among their countries.

Premier Arrat called his wife, Medina, into his quarters. He told her the good news and she immediately called the servants to prepare for a celebration. There would be many dignitaries of Terra attending. Leaders from around Terra and all the Arab Nations government officials were invited. Medina Arrat knocked on Jophiel's bedroom door and he told her to enter. She asked him if he had any special invitations to be sent for his party. He told her he wanted Gabriel and his father present. She gasped.

When Premier Arrat called Premier Analoff to invite him to the adoption celebration, Analoff accepted. He and Gabriel would certainly attend. This made Premier Arrat very proud of his adopted son. In such a short period of time, his son accomplished more than he could have done in a lifetime of negotiations.

The preparation for the party was overwhelming. Medina Arrat arranged to have the celebration in Cairo, at the Muhammad Ali Mosque, also called the Alabaster Mosque due to the prodigious use of the stone on the walls, both inside and out. It has dozens of crystal balls illuminating the interior hall where the party would be held. Breathtaking in its very nature, this Mosque was built in 1824 by Muhammad Ali Pasha, and its design follows the Nur al-Din Mosque in Istanbul by the Greek architect, Yousuf Boshna. The top chefs from all over Terra were hired to prepare their finest cuisine. Six hundred invitations were sent out to the most important dignitaries. The party was announced on a daily basis from every telecommunications center throughout Terra. The security alone was the best from the United Nations. Arrangements were made to invite David Penn, the most popular magician on Terra, to perform.

As the honored guests pulled up to the celebration, the 255-foot minarets and the dome of the Muhammad Ali Mosque peered out from behind the walls of the Citadel. Sited on the slope of the

Mukattam Hills, it commands a complete view of Cairo. The Citadel was constructed using stone taken from the many small pyramids at Gaza. They walked into the interior courtyard, where the walls of the Mosque gave the appearance of ageless mystery as the shadows cast by the afternoon sun. All guests were to place foot covers over their shoes before entering the place of worship, as was the custom.

David Penn, preparing for his act that was to take place in the theater structure across from the Mosque, began to feel uneasy. An odd feeling started nagging at him. Could this possibly be another encounter with an alien penguin? He shrugged. No, he was imagining it.

When Premier Analoff arrived with Gabriel, there was a complete hush over the enormous crowd. What miracle was bringing these two enemies together? Premier Arrat and Jophiel greeted Premier Analoff and Gabriel and escorted them to their table. The leaders of all the other countries were in awe as the ceremony began. Jophiel was overwhelmed by the love and warmth of everyone who traveled thousands of miles to extend their best wishes. After dinner, the guests were escorted to the theater. Everyone left the mosque and removed their shoe coverings and entered the theater.

Gabriel and Jophiel sat in the front row with their parents and the President of the United States and the Premier of Russia. The lights were dimmed to almost complete darkness. The audience was hushed and all attention was on the spotlight in the center of the stage.

When David Penn appeared, it was as if he descended from the ceiling. Everyone was so excited to see this acclaimed magician. They greeted him with a great applause. David felt a force so strong he felt his throat closing on him. When Gabriel looked up and saw David, he shuddered. This would be an event all of Terra would never forget. He whispered into Jophiel's ear, "This man is evil. He was at my bar mitzvah and showed his true identity. We must not let him harm anyone here." Jophiel looked up into the face of his guest entertainer. It was at that moment that David decided to challenge his enemies. He glanced down into the front row and, when he saw Gabriel, he shifted to the person next to him – Jophiel. He called Jophiel to the stage. Jophiel walked up slowly and David took off his cape and placed it around Jophiel's shoulders. He said to the audience, "Since this is a celebration, I have a special present for all of you here. Since everyone here knows Jophiel was adopted, but no one knows his true origin, I'll let you in on a secret. His true parents are aliens. They are not followers of Muhammad, and Arab blood does not flow through his veins. He is a complete imposter. I'll now reveal to you his true identity." The audience shifted in their seats, listening intently, for they were not sure if David was speaking in earnest or was about to mystify them with a special performance. Jophiel felt his muscles and veins throbbing. He felt his buttons popping off his shirt and his shoestrings bursting. His clothing flew off of him and his skin was replaced by thick white and gold fur and his penguin form was slowly being revealed. Everyone thought it was a trick. They stood and applauded. David then told Jophiel to tell everyone where he was from. Jophiel clung to his gold ring and, rubbing it, he reversed the spell. David started growing horns and his identity was slowly coming into focus. Gabriel ran up to the stage and, while rubbing his own gold ring, watched in horror as David Penn took on a satanic form. His shoes, popping off his feet, were replaced by huge hoofs. Gabriel asked him, "Who are you really, David?" David replied, "The greatest Archangel in heaven." Then he changed into a beautiful angel, the sight of which took the audience into a more realistic mode. They knew this was no trick. This was really happening in front of them, but they were aghast as David continued, "My goal is to tempt you humans into destroying yourselves. The Creator believes you are worth saving, whereas I believe you are, by nature, mice that need to be crushed to smithereens under my feet. You are not worthy of His love, and I will prove to Him I was right all along." David disappeared into thin air. Then Jophiel returned to his human form and the lights went on in the theater. Premier Arrat walked up to the stage and announced, "I have just seen with my own eyes the meaning of why we are all here today. As a Terra family, we must conquer the devil, not each other. No more wars and hate. Let us today vow to make a difference and bring Terra together as one loving family. Let us not take up arms against each other but pray to the one Creator of all to give us strength and faith to unite and become an enemy only with the one who wishes us harm, the devil himself."

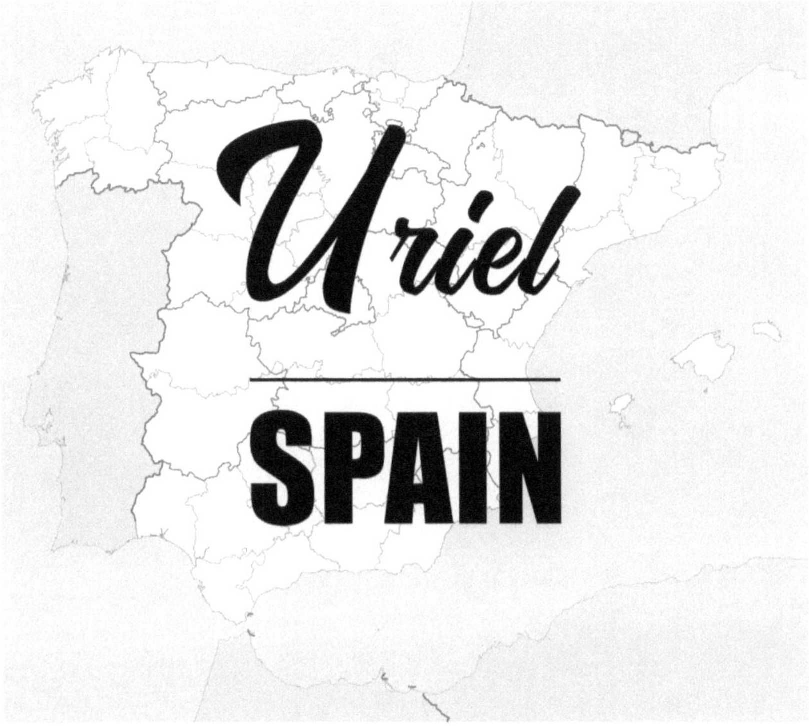
Uriel
SPAIN

Chapter Five

URIEL

Uriel peered out the spaceship window. The sky was dramatically bright in the early morning light over Madrid. It was his time to leave the familiarity of his vessel. Already the comforting covering of fur was gone, replaced by what was alien to him but necessary to his mission – his new appearance as a human. His pod was ejected 2,135 feet above the sea level of the Mediterranean. Uriel was spiraling downward toward a garden atop a rooftop.

He landed in the middle of this tranquil garden, which was surrounded with greens and vegetables. He was not hurt, as he had landed in a patch of soft shrubbery. He watched through the window overlooking the garden and saw a group of aliens pointing at him. They were all dressed the same. They came running out to see who this naked boy exiting from the pod was. They surrounded him and stared inquisitively. These were the Sisters of the Convent of the Royal Barefoot Carmelite Nuns. From the windows of the upper floors of the convent is a lovely view of the rooftop garden, where they have grown their own vegetables for centuries, unaffected by the bustling Gran Via, just one block north of the gigantic El Corte Ingles department store practically alongside. The sisters wrapped him in a blanket, asking him in Spanish who he was and what was his name. They led him down the grandiose stairways, lavishly decorated with frescoes and carved wood, art treasures by El Greco, Zurbarian, Titian, and Sanchez Coello, as well as Rubens tapestries. It was a retreat house for disconsolate empresses, queens, princesses and the very wealthy. And so it was that Maria Elana, Queen of Spain, was here.

The nuns put a blanket about him and took Uriel into the convent and brought him soup. They watched him curiously and felt he was not a threat. They asked him what religion he was. He told them there was only one Creator, one great power in the Universe. The sisters called their physician and asked him to check out Uriel physically and mentally. They asked him to bring clothing to the convent, for Uriel was completely naked under the blanket. The physician rushed over to the convent, bringing Uriel his scrubs, which were green cotton loose-fitting pants with a drawstring and a loose-fitting shirt he wore in the operating room. He had driven quickly through the crowded streets of Madrid, wondering who this boy could be. He was greeted at the convent door by Mother Superior. The doctor felt Uriel's pulse and took his blood pressure. He was in great physical form. His physique was above average. He looked like a professional athlete. He told the physician he could not remember his origin and the doctor decided he would have Uriel come into the hospital in a few days for some tests. Meanwhile, he would let him rest and receive some loving nurturing from the wonderful sisters. He dressed Uriel in his green scrubs and told him to follow the sisters' orders and that he would be back in a few days to arrange for him to come into the hospital.

Queen Maria Elana was in the private chapel praying for her special intention. She was a beautiful woman with much to be thankful for, but she was without child; she wanted a child of her own, one to carry the crown of her country. She prayed many novenas in vain for a baby of her own. Her husband was ruler over Spain. He told her if she did not give him a son then he would have to adopt one. Time was running out. She was 39 years old. Her physicians told her the chances were slim, since her husband was twenty years her senior. There in the small private chapel, she prayed for a miracle. Would the Creator please answer her only prayer? Why was she barren? She cried daily. The nuns placed her petition in front of the Blessed Mother of Guadalupe statue for continuous prayer. She herself had heard of the miracles of Guadalupe and felt deeply positive in her heart that the Blessed Mother would ask her divine Son that she conceive. The fasting and praying were all things Queen Maria Elana dared not stop, for if she did she would lose all hope.

In the main dining hall of the convent was a painting of "God the Father" hung by huge chains from the ceiling. It was painted by a Mexican nun and was considered a treasured work of art. The nuns brought Uriel to the table for dinner. As they escorted him to his chair, he gasped in disbelief. There in front of his eyes was his Creator who sent him to Terra, his portrait hanging suspended on chains. "My dear sisters," Uriel said, "behold your Creator." They looked up at the portrait. They looked back at him as he spoke, "I was sent here to save Terra. It is part of a mission my brothers and I volunteered for. The Creator believes in you humans and you should think of Him as your Father. He is the same Creator of all. I was sent here to bring love and peace. I have walked our gardens with Him. I have spoken with Him. My planet Pellisa has no evil. There is no death. Please help me gain some position where I can make a difference. They all thought he was delirious from his fall, as he spoke with such passion.

Queen Maria Elana walked out of the chapel slowly. As she

entered the dining hall, she felt faint. She called to one of the nuns to help her. She fainted in the dining hall doorway. The nun called to Uriel. He lifted the Queen and carried her to her small sparsely furnished room. He gently placed her on a single bed. Another nun rushed in with smelling salts. The Queen started coughing and Uriel held her hand. When she opened her eyes, she thought she was dreaming. She was looking into the eyes of a 17-year-old Spanish boy who had eyes exactly like her own. He could pass for her son. She asked him who he was. He said his name was Uriel, but he could not remember anything else. She called in the Mother Superior, who could tell her no more. Maria Elana told the nuns her prayer for a miracle was now in process. She said the Creator sent her Uriel. He was to be taken by limousine with her to Pacio de la Zarruela, on the outskirts of Madrid, where she and her husband, King Fernando VIII, resided.

They were escorted by the military for their trip to the Palace. The Queen always wore a black hat with a brim to shade her delicate blue-green eyes, with black lashes so thick you were mesmerized by her glare, and with fair skin and auburn hair, much admired by the Spanish. Her features were softly regal. When she smiled, a cherubic face became exquisite. She might pass for a young matron of nobility on a country picnic. For all her responsibilities, not to mention the discomforts of infertility, her composure was unruffled.

Graciously she welcomed the military escort sent by her husband, King Fernando, to guard her on every journey. In the limousine she advised the King by phone of her miracle of finding Uriel. He was very uneasy of having a stranger stay at his palace whom no one had investigated beforehand.

The King was waiting for the Queen. As she and Uriel entered the center hall, the King approached with a warm hug and smile for her. He flashed his handsome smile Uriel's way and was surprised at his poise. He looked like a Spanish prince who just returned from a week of sailing the Mediterranean Sea. The King questioned Uriel as to how he became a guest of the Nuns of the Carmelite Convent. Uriel asked if he could have a private talk with the King. The King brought Uriel into the library and sat him down. He told the butler to bring tea and cigars. As Uriel gazed at the King, he felt a sincere feeling of warmth. The King was six feet two inches tall and had salt and pepper hair and a beard to match. His skin was weather beaten from years of sailing, but that only added to his ruggedness. He was wearing a smoking jacket with an ascot. He was very regal in manner, yet there was a hint of tenderness. Uriel tried to relax and find a way to begin his story. The butler brought in the tea and cigars. The King handed one to Uriel and then lit one himself. Uriel told him he did not know how to smoke. The King showed him how. They sipped their tea and smoked their cigars, which helped Uriel relax somewhat.

The King sat back in his large cushioned chair in front of the fireplace and told Uriel to begin his explanation of his origin. Uriel told the King it was the Creator's plan for him to land at the Convent and to be accepted by Spanish Royalty. The King listened dubiously. Uriel was either a spy or crazy! He told him to proceed with who the Creator was. Uriel told the King, "I am from the planet Pellisa. The Creator is the one who made all the Universe. He is the Supreme Being who designed every living creature and there is no other greater than Him. The Carmelite Sisters have a painting of the Creator in their dining hall. I told them briefly my intention here on Terra was to stop this planet from destroying itself by a nuclear disaster. My other five brothers are living with government heads of state in five other countries, and we are all on a mission of love. You, King Fernando, will play a great part in this mission. I am from a planet 400 billion light years from Terra. My galaxy was the first created and your galaxy the last. Your planet,

Terra, is the only one that has evil and inhabitants who destroy each other. If you need reassurance, I will show you my true form before I metamorphosed into a human." The King, totally convinced Uriel was a psychopath of some sort, leaned back in his lounge chair, drew on his cigar, and said, "By all means, Uriel, let me see your true physical form."

Uriel stood up and walked over towards the fireplace. He looked like a young medical student with his green scrubs and white buck shoes. He took the gold ring off his finger and started to rub it intensely. He closed his eyes and began praying for the Creator to help him prove his identity. He felt his chest expanding rapidly. His white fur was popping out of everywhere. He watched as his shoes flew off his feet and his webbed, three-pointed flipper ones were in full view. His arms were turned into wings and his nose was replaced by his full yellow shadings. The King was shaken and frightened. He sat back on the lounge chair. He could not speak. Uriel sensed the King's fear and metamorphosed back to his human state. He picked up his clothing and began getting dressed. The King, still shaking, asked Uriel what his intentions were with the Queen and himself. Uriel said he hoped to be adopted and to be granted enough power to negotiate with other heads of state on the Planet Terra to bring peace and love and equality.

The King called his butler into the room. He asked that the Queen be brought to him at once. His heart was pounding. Could this boy be the reason his wife had not conceived? He knew, if he adopted him, it would make Uriel the immediate Prince of Spain. He knew also there would be a tremendous investigation of the origin of Uriel. He reasoned that, if this were the Creator's wishes, he would leave it all in His hands. After all, He was the Creator of the Universe.

As the Queen entered the room, she saw her King as she never before did. He was so flushed that she thought he must be ill. She ran over to him and sat beside him. He told Uriel to come over to him. Uriel walked over and stood in front of the King and Queen of Spain. The King took the Queen's hand and told Uriel to kneel down in front of them both. He did so and he told the Queen to place her left hand on Uriel's shoulder as the King placed his right hand on Uriel's other shoulder. He said to his wife, "Behold your son, my Queen, and Uriel, behold your parents. My Queen, this is our son, the new Prince of Spain." The Queen dropped down on her knees and prayed a prayer of thanks to her beloved Blessed Mother, whom she was sure asked Jesus her Savior to grant her most desired wish. They all held hands and bowed their heads and prayed silently, thanking the Creator for this special gift to them.

Adoption arrangements were to take place immediately. The King and Queen invited Presidents and Kings and Ambassadors from around Terra for the newly ordained Prince of Spain's coronation.

The King and Queen privately adopted Uriel, then flew with him to the southern town of Spain called Seville for a private weekend to get to know each other. It was hardly private, as thousands of Spaniards thronged the streets of the southern city as they rode in a limousine with guards on motorcycles enveloped on all sides. The orange blossoms were beginning to perfume the air, and it was for the King and Queen a rejuvenating experience to have a family at last.

They walked up the steps of Seville's Gothic Cathedral and went in and each said a private prayer of thanks. They were photographed thousands of times on their three-day stay. Upon returning home, they prepared vigorously for Uriel's coronation.

The King planned to give Uriel precedence over any close relative as pretender to the Spanish throne. He had the Prime Minister of the government and the Secretary General of PSOE (Spanish Workers Socialist Party) meet with Uriel on a steady basis to familiarize themselves with their new future leader. Uriel became engrossed in the regional and local governments. He would walk the streets alone sometimes and introduce himself to the poorer citizens, asking them what they needed for a better way of life. He was often seen among the poorer fishing regions of the northwest boarding the vessels and mingling with the working class fishermen, who would provide him with their most intimate thoughts and desires for bettering the economy and the way of life for their people. The word of Uriel's coronation was heard all over Terra. The heads of state from every walk of life on Terra were invited to this extraordinary event. The newspapers and television news shows, unable to explain how this boy could come out of the blue and somehow become the new Prince of Spain, led the media to concoct their own stories. He was a mystery to everyone. Only the Nuns of the Carmelite Cloister order knew how he arrived here, and they honored their vow of silence.

Uriel and his new mother were asked by the King to dedicate the new U.S. designed Santa Maria guided missile frigate submarine, with standard SM-1 surface-to-air missile, in memory of the deceased members of the Navy. When they arrived, the Naval officers escorted them aboard and took them to the lower deck. Uriel asked if he and his mother could observe the operation of how the submarine descends the surface.

The officer brought them to a telescope so they could watch the sub dive below the sea. This was the first time the Queen was aboard a sub and she was both thrilled and scared. The dive was one of many the ship had made in her preliminary exercises. This, however, was the first with anyone not of the Navy aboard. The water seemed to top the telescope in mere seconds, and the Queen, expecting to get a bit of seasickness, felt nothing. It was as if they were not moving. The officer watched as his Queen held onto the telescope and stared into the window of it as if she were watching a thrilling movie. Uriel asked the officer to stop the sub on the ocean floor. He noticed a look of surprise on the officer's face. He told Uriel that this was not one of the maneuvers that they had tested.

Uriel urged him on. The officer was apprehensive. What if the gears were not shifting? What if there was a problem? With the Queen and the future Prince of Spain on board, he could not take the chance. He told Uriel they could arrange that another time. Uriel spoke very authoritatively. "Do as I command, your Queen and I are ready." The officer called some of his crew together and prepared to have them stop the ship. They were stunned, but none of them dared argue. The ship was then made to descend to the ocean floor.

Queen Maria Elana watched the Naval officers working frantically at the large operational equipment. She and Uriel were both very excited. The ship took only minutes, it seemed, before all the engines were quieted. The descent went smoothly. The crew, the Queen and Uriel watched with eager eyes as the fish swam by and the ocean's floor was clear and real as if one were walking around it on the outside. The Queen was fascinated and told them they were brave men and she was privileged to be their Queen. They were elated. Uriel told them the same and thanked the Officer in Charge for making the daring move. Then Uriel asked them to ascend. The officer pushed several buttons and gears and waited calmly for the computer to register "ascending." Instead, a red light flashed across the computer screen and the words "engine failure" came on. Once more, he repeated the same procedure. Again the red light words "engine failure" appeared. How could he call for assistance and not alert everyone? He picked up the complicated telesystem receiver and heard not a sound. He pushed two other systems - nothing! He was now in a complete state of panic. He called his two highest officers to the operational panel. They were not able to override the system failures. There was no movement. He finally told the Queen and Uriel. Uriel told the officer to gather all the crew. They all listened as Uriel told them not to panic. He asked about the oxygen supply on hand—the figure was not good and the emergency generator of oxygen was also not working. For Uriel, there was only one answer: he had to reveal his true identity. He would not put the

Queen in harm's way. She alone here knew his true identity. He whispered to his mother, "I love you very much. I must do this for our lives and theirs. We will ask the Creator to bless us."

Uriel took the gold ring the Creator gave him on Pellisa and placed it on his finger. He gathered the crew around him and told him he could bring help to them. They all thought he was crazy. Then he told them he was sent to Terra for a purpose by the Creator. The Spanish crew watched in disbelief as Uriel transformed into a white and gold fur penguin. His tailored suit was now lying on the sub's floor. His shoes were flung ten feet away and his webbed feet were towering a foot off the ground. They were all in shock. He asked where the closest hatch was located for his exit. The exit hatch door opened and Uriel started his swim towards land. As he was getting closer to land, there was a scuba diving course in process and the students were all diving for the first time. They had their underwater tanks on and some had underwater cameras. As Uriel flew through the sea, two scuba students were filming the coral reef and the many species of fish they encountered on their first expedition. All of a sudden, coming into view was Uriel. They all gasped into their mouthpieces as he flew by them with great speed. What was that? They quickly surfaced and breathlessly told their scuba teacher they saw a 200-pound penguin with white and gold fur fly by them at an enormous speed. The teacher told them they probably did not decompress properly and they needed oxygen. He said that all sixteen species of penguin live south of the equator, not off the coast of Spain. They had to be in a fever state. The students were positive of what they saw and could not wait to develop the film one of the students had taped with his underwater camera.

When Uriel was approaching the shore, he realized he would still be in penguin form. How could he metamorphose back to human and walk around unclothed? He noticed a sail ship out about a mile and decided to swim to it. When he came up to the surface, he saw several couples lying on the boat sunbathing. He metamorphosed back to human and swam to the ship. He asked someone to radio the Navy and gave them a code. He said a submarine was in distress and needed immediate emergency assistance. They insisted he come on board. Uriel told them he would wait in the water until they made contact. They were wary of him, but they agreed to do as he asked. The Naval officer receiving the message was elated. He had been trying to make contact with the sub for half an hour. Where was the location? Uriel told them where the sub was and then disappeared under the water. They watched for him to surface for air. They picked up binoculars and looked in all directions. Puzzled and curious, they decided to set their sails in the directions given to the Naval officer. Most of their crew had been drinking and their alcohol level was advanced. Consequently, they went off course.

Uriel immediately changed back to penguin form so he could fly under the waters. He made it back to the ship within minutes. He swam into the hatch on the sub and walked into a room where the crew and the Queen were waiting. The Queen was so excited to see Uriel, she shrieked with happiness. The crew was still in awe at the story their Queen had just revealed about Uriel. They watched Uriel in penguin form pick up his clothing and go into the office, where he metamorphosed back to human. They were secretly afraid of him. The Queen asked them all to promise not to reveal what they had seen. With the arrival of help, the sub was soon back on course.

The King was at the Palace preparing for Uriel's coronation as Prince of Spain. He wanted the most popular entertainer and magician presently on Terra—that would be David Penn. The King called the famous magician personally and David accepted without hesitation. The King arranged for millions of Spaniards and royal watchers around the world to watch the coronation via live broadcasts and arranged for 14,000 spectators at Seville's bullring for a performance by the Royal Equestrian School and then the performance of David Penn. This coronation would be viewed by almost all of the countries on Terra. The Spaniards considered this one of the most prominent coronations in the history of Spain. They never saw their country come together so overwhelmingly for one political figure. Uriel's sudden presence and their Queen's miracle for a son touched the hearts of everyone.

When the day of the coronation finally arrived, Uriel was quite nervous. He asked the Queen to assist him at dressing and then to review his vows and rehearse the coronation procedures with him. Uriel looked like a handsome Spanish Prince in his white tuxedo with his blue-black hair and tanned skin. His chiseled features and six-foot frame, perfect from head to toe, would turn any head.

David Penn arrived in Seville the night before the coronation. In the morning, he walked over to the bullring to investigate where he would be performing. He felt a little quiver, held his stomach, and felt it again when he took another step forward. It was a familiar quiver, one that terrified him. Nothing ever terrified him, except, of course, his recent experiences with the aliens. How could this possibly be? He was in Seville preparing for a performance of the newly coronated Prince of Spain. He took a couple of deep breaths and walked on. The stage hands were setting up various areas for the coronation, the bullfight and the magical show. David introduced himself and was happy to be recognized. Many asked for his autograph. He obliged, and everyone was most helpful. David handed them a list of his preferences for the stage set-ups and all the props he needed for his performance. He had three hours to get himself prepared.

The Royal Family set off for the airport and their private jet to head for Seville. The bullring was set up for the coronation first, which was to be privately attended by most of the leaders on Terra. When the first family entered the gates, the overwhelming silence of the enormous crowd was strange. All who were invited to this coronation were still very much confused as to the origin of Uriel.

The stage was set with three thrones and an altar. The government officials of Spain and the Archbishop were waiting patiently. The King and Queen entered with Uriel and the crowds stood up and cheered. The Archbishop kissed them and the ceremony began. The king placed a crown on Uriel's head and put a ring on his finger and said to the people, "You have come from around all of Terra to honor my son, and I am privileged to have you. To all my countrymen, here is your new Prince and future King Uriel." There was a roar as the crowds rose to their feet and cheered for thirty minutes. Uriel walked up to the microphone and told the crowd, "Bless you all. I thank you for traveling from distant lands on Terra to celebrate my coronation. I will do my best to be your political servant and to bring all of Spain together as one family. My main objective as your Prince will be to bring peace to all of Terra. May I say that there are four danger zones in human life that can cause unlimited trouble if they get out of hand: force, wealth, sex and speech. The animal life contains these as well. Two scarcely surface as problems at all. The spoken word does not, for animals cannot communicate enough to seriously deceive. Neither really does wealth, for to become a serious social problem the drive for possessions requires foresight and sustained greed at levels unknown in the animal kingdom. As for sex and force, they too pose no serious problems. Periodicity keeps sex from becoming obsessive, and in-built restrainings hold violence in check. With the curious exception of ants, intra-special warfare is seldom found. Where it has broken out, the species has usually destroyed itself. With human beings, things are different. Jealousies, hatreds, and revenge can lead to violence that, unless checked, rips communities to pieces. Murder instigates blood feuds that drag on indefinitely. Sex, if it violates certain restraints, can rouse passions so intense as to destroy entire communities, similarly with theft and prevarication. We can imagine societies in which people do exactly as they please on these counts, but none have been found and anthropologists have now covered Terra. Apparently, if total permissiveness has ever been tried, its inventors have not survived for anthropologists to study.

"I must tell you, my family on Terra, that in the beginning the Creator made the heavens and Terra. This, my brothers and sisters, can be proven in your own individual lives if you turn to the Creator. Everyone must look at his brother and sister, regardless of color or creed, and love them. I ask all of you to look into your own hearts and, if there lies a prejudice, ask your Father in heaven to remove it. Please listen to my message. The whole of Terra will be lost forever if hatred and wars persist. This is my plea to all of you. Please love each other and sacrifice your prejudices to the Creator. He is there in your hearts, all of you. No Terra being is less valued in the Creator's sight. Please enjoy the festivities of the day." They whispered to one another, "He is a prophet, not a Prince." The King and Queen were so overwhelmed with love for their son, they sobbed tears of joy. The King and Queen spoke to the crowd. They told everyone to listen to their son's message and all of Terra would know peace.

Meanwhile, David the magician was in the room with the matador, joking about his upcoming magical tricks he was about to entertain the crowd with. The matador asked David if he wanted to join the bullfight and mix in something that would make the crowd excited. David got a brainstorm. He told the matador to leave everything to him.

The bullring was bustling with excitement. The crowds stood and cheered frantically. The matador stood six-feet three-inches tall and commanded the attention of all the females. He was extraordinary when it came to stage presence. He danced around the bullring and the crowds began to get more and more emotional. The bull dashed onto the ring and the size of him was frightening.

The Royal Equestrian School students were all wondering if they would ever be able to perform with such elegance. The bull was now ready for the final quest. He kicked his hoofs several times in back of him and his nostrils were pointed directly at the matador, whose red satin cape was now dangling under his left arm, and the crowd was hushed. As the bull started to charge, David placed a spell on the bull and he disappeared completely. Everyone kept looking around the ring for the bull to appear again. Finally, David walked into the ring and over to the matador. They embraced and everyone started to cheer. David then took the matador's red cape and placed it over his arm. He walked several yards to the middle of the ring and started to swing the cape. The bull appeared and started to lick David's hand. The crowd roared with laughter, and then David summoned Uriel. Uriel walked out onto the ring. David started to get shaky—he knew the feeling and was deathly leery of it. He asked Uriel to take the cape and summon the bull. David stepped back and the matador whispered to David that it was too dangerous. David told him he had total control and he and the matador walked off the ring. Uriel started to swing the cape to the left and right and the bull started to charge. Uriel was making all the proper moves and David was beginning to figure out Uriel's true origin. He would just let the bull take care of the Prince.

The matador was without a sword. The crowd was speechless. The bull was charging with a vengeance to kill. Uriel was in deep trouble. The King and Queen began to shout to stop the bull. Uriel rubbed his ring and immediately started to metamorphose back into penguin form. He elevated ten feet above the ground and the bull was running around in circles. The crowd roared. They thought it to be a joke and magic act with the perfect timing of a professional. They were elated. The King and Queen knew the truth but stood in silence, relieved their precious Uriel was safe. The matador came into the ring with the sword and Uriel metamorphosed back to human. He quickly picked up his clothing and got dressed. The matador stood beside Uriel and placed the sword into his hand. He placed his own hand on Uriel's and the bull came charging. Uriel and the matador pointed the sword down to the ground and the bull fell asleep in the middle of the ring. The crowd went wild. It was the most spectacular celebration ever witnessed in their country.

Hanael
CHINA

Chapter Six

HANAEL

Hanael was now alone in the spaceship. His five brothers being gone from their cabins made Hanael feel lonely. He closed his eyes and prayed he could join his family very soon. He felt something was about to happen. He stood up and looked at his legs. He was in the middle of metamorphosing. His webbed feet were now forming toes and his wings were now human arms. He reached for his face and felt the moisture of sweat for the first time. His sweat was now frozen on his goosebumps and he longed for his thick fur to keep him warm. He felt the vibration of the cabin's door and, as it opened, he saw the densely massed blue and white clouds covering the planet Terra. He was flying over the Xinjiang-Mongolian Uplands in the northwestern part of China. There were deserts and rugged mountains that looked as barren as some of the moons he had just witnessed. He knew as he flew closer to Terra through the clouds that life here was bustling. The farmlands were bursting with rice crops and wheat crops and the farmers were tending their soil.

Hanael's ship closed in on Beijing, the capital of China. Po-Linn was the most powerful person in the Communist Party and served as chairman of both the Communist Party and the Central Military of the government. His wife, Yu-Chen, was his oxygen. He made no decision until he reviewed it with her. It was not commonly known that she actually made the most powerful decisions. Pu-Linn and Yu-Chen were childless. Yu-Chen was not concerned that her husband would leave her due to this, as most Chinese men would, because she knew he could not survive without her wisdom. They were on a tour of the villages and small towns outside of Beijing when they noticed people in the rice fields pointing up to the sky. Yu-Chen looked up and saw a human figure actually falling through the clouds. She rubbed her eyes in disbelief!

Hanael was free-falling and landed in a flood rice field in the Yangtze Valley, which forms the southern part of the Eastern Lowlands. The farmers found Hanael's naked body covered in mud, lying lifeless in the field. A young farmer was right next to Hanael when he landed and thought he must have been skydiving and lost his parachute in mid-air.

Yu-Chen Linn told her husband to direct the driver towards the spot where all the commotion was. As they drew closer, Yu-Chen realized the body she saw flying through the air was lying in the middle of this rice paddy. She jumped out of the limousine and ran over to the crowds and saw Hanael. She started giving him mouth-to-mouth resuscitation. Yu-Chen, on seeing Hanael starting to breathe, ordered a farmer to take off his shirt and wrap it around Hanael's naked body. The limousine driver was ordered to carry Hanael into the car. Pu-Linn watched in amazement as Yu-Chen told him they were taking Hanael home with them. He gave her no argument. The farmers could not believe how Yu-Chen had so much authority and the leader of their country listened to her orders, but they were touched by her tenderness and watched as the limousine pulled away.

Hanael was shaken. He watched through the limousine windows as the Red Chinese Army was practicing their drills in front of their capital. Yu-Chen Linn instructed the limousine driver to bring Hanael to the guest room next to her quarters. She climbed the stairs towards Hanael's room with so much anxiety. She comforted him and held his hand and proceeded to ask him questions with newly felt maternal instincts.

Hanael looked into Yu-Chen's eyes and remembered his own mother's loving glances back on Pellisa. He felt Yu-Chen was good and was not going to harm him, and yet he was not sure of what the consequences would be if he reported to her his true origin. Yu-Chen asked him if he was a spy. Hanael, not knowing where her thoughts were based, said yes, he was a spy for the Creator. Yu-Chen was puzzled, being brought up only with Communism as her government and her God. She knew of the Buddhism beliefs that her ancestors occasionally spoke of when she was young. Never having the proper books to study his teaching, she just lived as instructed by her government. She asked Hanael to explain to her what country his Creator was from and why he was in China. Hanael took a deep breath and replied, "Your planet Terra has been plagued with many diseases and death. I was sent here by the Creator of not only your planet but of all planets, stars and Universes. He has tried many times to bring peace here, but somehow greed and lust prevail. He sent Terra Moses, Jesus, Siddhartha Guatama, Mahatma Gandhi and Muhammed to bring the message that love of brotherhood in man is the only way to a life of peace, and yet it is filled with hatred and greed. The Creator sent me and five of my brothers from a planet called Pellisa, billions of light years from here, to live in different countries and prove to the inhabitants of Terra that you are all one family. This cannot be done by force and weapons. All must come to an understanding that, if we take care of our brothers in every corner of Terra, no greed will be able to poison man's heart. My mission is to convince you and your husband to agree to letting your people be free to practice religion and honor their Creator. He is here for you and your government and your people. Let them have their independence and freedom." Yu-Chen answered, "The religions you speak of also fight wars and bring death to their people. The free nations fight amongst one another, so how can you defend freedom when it has proven not to be the answer? We try to give all families the same. They do not complain. They can be secure in knowing they will eat and have a roof over their heads if they obey the government and follow the rules."

Hanael was now at a loss for words. What was he to do? So he asked Yu-Chen if she believed in one Creator, perhaps then her outlook would be different. She told Hanael she only believed in her surroundings at the moment. He told her he was living proof that this Creator existed. She told him she saw only a delirious Chinese boy. He in turn told her to watch him closely. Hanael rubbed the gold ring and began his metamorphose. Yu-Chen watched in amazement as Hanael's body took on the body of the white and gold furry penguin and his clothes burst off his body. As he stood in front of her, she for the first time glimpsed faith other than her government. She held out her hand and Hanael held it for a moment, then gasped as the door opened. Pu-Linn was standing alone in the doorway. He said nothing as he walked toward his wife and this furry penguin. Yu-Chen took Pu-Linn's hand and told him to sit down next to her. She then told Hanael to become a boy again. As the fur evaporated into human skin and the arms and legs were forming, Pu-Linn became extremely frightened. He jumped off the sofa and began yelling for the guards. Yu-Chen stopped him and told him she had made a great discovery that would help him conquer Terra. He gasped, wide-eyed, as he watched Hanael become the Chinese boy from the rice paddy.

Hanael explained to the head of the Communist Party of China the truth of his mission. Pu-Linn had a hard time comprehending, since he never believed there was a Creator. He asked what he could do, and Hanael told him to adopt him and let him follow the course of his mission. When he nodded yes, Yu-Chen was so happy that she finally had her own son.

They agreed to adopt Hanael and he was given a position working as an assistant to Pu-Linn in the Central Military Commission of the Government. When members of his party questioned him of Hanael's presence here, Pu-Linn explained Hanael was a distant nephew whose family was killed by an earthquake while visiting Turkey and he had promised to raise him in the event of their death. No one questioned the most powerful man in China. Yu-Chen taught Hanael the history of China and showed him poor areas and spoke of prisons filled with political prisoners, some of whom were teenagers like himself. Hanael made one of his goals working to give freedom to these people and to release the innocent from the chains of prison.

Pu-Linn arranged for an adoption of Hanael. He invited all heads of the Communist countries on Terra, and this included the Premier of Russia. He knew that Terra must come together as one family and that if he invited the capitalists there would be an immediate revolution in China. He figured he would start by uniting the Communist party and then let Hanael proceed with his mission. When the Russian Premier told Raphael they were planning a trip to China – for the head of that country was to adopt a son – Raphael immediately knew the boy was his brother Hanael.

All arrangements were made for the adoption ceremony. The Central Military Commission arranged for the entertainment. The best magician on Terra was contacted and asked to make a personal appearance. Since they were gracious enough to let him walk through the historical Great Wall of China, he willingly accepted. The arrangements were made and the ceremony was to take place in the middle of Tiananmen Square, where so many young students lost their lives when they protested a lack of freedom of speech.

Hanael knew it was here that he needed to make a connection for the whole of Terra to come together as one family.

Preparation for Hanael's adoption was hectic. He had little time to explore the prisons or poor sections he wanted so much to change. He awoke at 3 in the morning the week before the adoption was to take place and decided to take a ride through Peking. He approached the main guard and asked for a vehicle. He was still in his pajamas and the guard dared not ask questions. Hanael took a map from the glove compartment and saw where the prison was located. He drove several hours until he finally reached his destination. He was hot and hungry as he pulled up to the prison gate and announced himself. The guard was not at all impressed. He figured this character was drunk. He called for assistance. The newly arrived guards immediately recognized Hanael. They let him in and asked whom it was he wished to visit. Hanael told them to let him have free reign. He took a set of keys for the entire complex and began his prison tour without the guards' assistance.

The first hallway had one hanging light bulb that was blinking on and off, casting a shadow on the walls from the cell bars enclosing at least one hundred prisoners. As Hanael approached the first cell, there was a stench he never before experienced. It actually made him choke. He walked up to the cell and could not believe his eyes. Two skeletal figures were asleep on the floor with nothing but what appeared to be a diaper on their bodies. Their faces were so thin that Hanael was unsure of their age. He ran to locate the nearest guard. The guard told Hanael that this entire section was only students from the revolt at Tiananmen Square in 1989 when they tried to take over the government. Hanael had already done his homework on the entire revolution. He believed the students had a right to be heard and the government should have listened to their request for equal rights and a chance to be included in participating in a voice for the population. He ordered the guards to bring him as many charged spotlights as they could find. Hanael placed the spotlights at strategic spots down the hallway where the students were actually dying and proceeded to turn on every last one of them. He walked up and down, announcing to them that he was there to free them of their injustices. They were all blinded by the lights. None of them had seen the light of day for years. They were all disoriented and without any hope. Hanael called Pu-Linn and told him he needed permission to free the students. Pu-Linn then placed a call to the main office at the prison and told him to wake up the head of security. Hanael called for several buses to transport all the students to his residence at the Palace. He did not trust the staff at the hospitals. He managed to have 146 students brought into his mansion and called the best doctors in China to evaluate each one of them. He set up a hospital ward with beds and made sure they received individual attention. They were all near death. Hanael tended to their needs personally. He felt as if he were actually their brother. He notified all of their families to visit. This did much to help and they all appeared to grow increasingly healthier.

Hanael set up a gym and a cafeteria where they could eat any time they wanted and he would hold a press conference, something unheard of in China, to tell the world how China was going to change their policy and have their people vote for a democracy, if that is what they wanted. Hanael was gaining popularity with all the younger Chinese in the entire continent.

Hanael's adoption was in full preparation and he was delighted to hear that David Penn, the world renowned magician, would be part of the entertainment. Hanael's future father had a guest room prepared in the mansion for the magician. David asked that he be near the family so he could get a feeling for their culture for his magic act. When David's limousine pulled in front of the Chinese mansion, he felt that uneasy sensation again. He convinced himself it was jetlag and his imagination. As David entered the guestroom, he noticed a letter on the bed. He started to read the welcome note from Hanael, and all of a sudden his brows became coated with sweat. His hands were quivering and his body became clammy. He knew the feeling well. He knew also he was far from the United States and Russia and Spain and Israel and Palestine. He was thoroughly convinced one of the aliens was very close by. He placed the welcome note back on the bed. The phone began to ring, and David trembled as he lifted the receiver. Hanael welcomed him to his home and thanked him for his time traveling across the whole of Terra to entertain at his adoption. As David spoke to Hanael, he brushed away beads of perspiration. He asked Hanael if he would mind if he took a nap for an hour before meeting with him. Hanael sent a servant to David's room to attend all of his needs for the duration of his stay. David laid down on the bed and gazed up at the cathedral ceiling. He felt deeply troubled. The butler arrived and asked David how he could best serve him for the next few days. David looked intensely into the servant's eyes. He told the servant to leave him alone for a half-hour and that he would then want a massage. The servant, sensing David may be feeling ill, asked if he needed a physician. David was beside himself. Could he really look that bad? He abruptly commanded the servant to leave. He finally laid down and began to piece the puzzle together.

Hanael found his future father in his library and asked if he could request the presence of a few special guests at his adoption. He requested from Pu-Linn that he be allowed to bring his five brothers to China for the event. He told Pu-Linn that it was part of his plan for Terra's unity. Pu-Linn, remembering how Hanael looked when metamorphosing, immediately agreed. He had his meeting with the Central Military Commission and told them he was going to invite the heads of five countries and their adopted sons. It would be part of the unification for the whole of Terra to recognize a brotherhood that could be universal. They all thought he had gone mad. The very core of their government was keeping their country separate from the others. They argued, but could not win. Yu-Chen told her husband it would all work out due to Hanael's intense connection with the universal Creator. The interpreter put a call through to all five governments and Pu-Linn himself invited them.

With all the changes taking place, the Central Military Commission held numerous private meetings without including their leader. They feared he would let the country be taken over by the Western Civilization culture and knew he would win out if he had a democratic vote for the country. They were conspiring to either assassinate him or use their nuclear power to destroy the five countries invited to their homeland. As they secretly met and debated, Pu-Linn knew something was not right with his comrades. They tried to be themselves, but were highly unsuccessful. One of the top security officials warned Pu-Linn his life was in danger.

All the invitations to the heads of the five countries and their adopted sons were confirmed. It was such an event of historical nature that the universal press was referring to it as an adoption of the United Nations as opposed to a singular Chinese adoption. For the first time in history, the top nations on Terra were going to be under the same roof. Hanael requested that the night before the adoption Pu-Linn arrange for all five of his brothers and their famous political fathers be together for a private dinner.

David could not sleep. His emotions were so high he felt he was literally going to explode. The masseuse was massaging him when David turned his head to look at the masseuse with piercing eyes and asked him what he knew of the adoption that was unusual. The masseuse watched David as his brows became wrinkled and his skin started to turn a gray color. He told David rumor had it that five nations had rulers that recently adopted sons the same age and that all of them were invited to the ceremony. David felt so weak he was faint. He asked the masseuse, "Are they from the United States, Israel, Palestine, Spain and Russia?" The masseuse replied, "You obviously knew already." David screamed for the masseuse to leave. He sat there and shook uncontrollably. All six brothers would definitely contribute to his destruction. He would have to think of a plan to destroy them very quickly. But how? They had powers beyond his and together they would surely let all of Terra in on who he truly was. He would have to ask for assistance from his satanic army.

Hanael could not wait to see his brothers. He watched the clock. They would all be arriving within the next few hours. He was so excited. Security was everywhere. Outside the palace looked like a sea of humanity. All six countries had hundreds of secret services lining the drive from the airport to the Palace. Six different nationalities blended the streets of Beijing into a United Nations. The air was electrified and all the hushed rumors about the coincidence of all six leaders adopting sons the same age made for an overwhelming feeling of spectacular proportions. Something of a tremendous change on Terra was happening.

Tiananmen Square was decorated for the celebration. All the flags of the six countries present were blowing in the wind. A sight never before imagined. The stage was set for the signing of the adoption papers to be witnessed by all, then a speech by both Pu-Linn and Hanael, followed by David Penn's magical acts.

Hanael was now getting dressed for his private dinner with his five brothers and their famous political fathers. He was just about ready when his mother entered the room. She sat on his bed and told him the guests had all arrived for the private dinner and that his father was very nervous. Hanael assured her that everything was fine. Yu-Chen told Hanael that the dining room was set and that she thought all the brothers should meet privately without anyone else present. Hanael thanked Yu-Chen for all she had done so far to help their mission and kissed her cheek and hugged her. Yu-Chen watched with pride as Hanael walked down the hallway into the grand dining room.

All his brothers were huddled in a circle with their arms around one another. Hanael ran up to them with tears in his eyes. The emotion was overwhelming. All of them looked at each other in amazement. They all resembled each other, yet their features were that of their given nationality. They each took turns relaying what they had accomplished for their mission on Terra. When they spoke of David the magician, all of them remembered how they had to use their gold ring to rescue themselves from his terrors. Hanael told the brothers he had not yet experienced David's evil, but that he was staying right upstairs, waiting to perform at his adoption. The brothers agreed they must stop David from ruining the adoption and get rid of him once and for all.

All of the famous political fathers arrived and the servants started serving the first course. The silence was evident and the boys realized the language barrier was the reason. They, in turn, interpreted all the six different languages. Pu-Linn raised his champagne glass and toasted them. "Thank all of you for your pilgrimage to my country. We are about to embark on an event of universal change. Our adopted sons are sent here by our only Creator, from the planet Pellisa, to unite our planet Terra in love and peace. We must have faith in their beliefs. We must let our sons now speak." Hanael stood up and asked his brothers to do the same. They stood and bowed their heads in prayer while Michael, the first born, spoke. "As all six of you leaders of the greatest countries on Terra have made room in your family for myself and my brothers, I must tell you the Creator has already done that for every human in heaven, as a loving father does for his beloved children. Only He loves unconditionally. Man thinks of himself as solid. He lives within an envelope of flesh and blood that is penetrated by his consciousness. Consciousness must be regarded as man's connection with his Source, his Creator, and its flexibility as man's greatest asset; yet when wrongly used, it is his greatest weakness. The consciousness of humanity today is so easily influenced by banal and barbaric doings that the magnificent cosmic purpose heaven has prepared in the creation of man is seldom recognized even minutely. Our Creator loves you humans on Terra so much that he sent us from Pellisa to teach you of love and to bring a better understanding of universal brotherhood. As I speak to you now, there is a plot to kill Pu-Linn and to terminate most of Terra. We must see to it that this is brought to an end immediately."

David Penn was indeed plotting for the destruction of Terra. He saw the Chinese government heads in their private chambers discussing the moment they would launch their nuclear warheads upon the main cities of Terra, destroying mostly the entire civilization. He cringed at the thought that these beasts, who call themselves men, would be the only living humans left on Terra. Then he thought again how it would be better off without most men, and so he would plot to destroy the Chinese and bring death to them, the same way he delivered evil to the Greeks and the Romans and the Persians and the Egyptians and the Pakistanis and the Babylonians. He remembered contributing to the destruction of Atlantis and Lemuria and Mu and Endria, the continents existing before they died under the waters in the Great Flood. David grinned in delight for the remembrance of the old Terra underwater, which he claims as his own doing through their own free will. Now he will watch her burning in her own fire.

Hanael knew where the largest television communication station was located. Although the Chinese population was not permitted free access to world news, by TV or the Internet, there were ways to connect the universal air waves to allow an international broadcast.

Hanael drove his five brothers to the television studio and entered the main room, where he could communicate to most of the free world and also his Chinese brothers who had access to a television and iPhones.

He strode through the station floor, and the television crew there bowed their heads slightly as he passed. They entered a room with ceiling to floor computers and Hanael turned the correct generator dials to bring about the change from local to international reception. All the shows airing at that time in all the countries on Terra were interrupted simultaneously with the warning words, "Emergency Broadcast." All six penguin brothers looked into the camera. Michael spoke, "My brothers on Terra, I am Michael Moroni, son of the Supreme Court Justice of the United States of America. This is an extreme emergency. Please listen carefully. I stand here with my five brothers. I am sure many millions of you recognize them. We came here to Terra for a mission to save this planet from self-destruction. I am broadcasting from Beijing, China. This country is in the process of setting off nuclear warheads to our major cities on Terra. There are a lot of you who believe in a Supreme Creator. There are many of you who believe you are the only living creatures in existence. May I inform you that there indeed is a Supreme Being and that He created all of you equally and in His image. There also exists an evil one, who is responsible for tempting you and, because of him, your free will has caused you despair. Right now we are going to fight a war predicted in Revelation in the Bible. A war with David Penn, an evil one who disguises himself as a magician among men. He is world-renowned and for this reason has made his way into all major governments. He is here in Beijing presently and trying to set off nuclear warheads. In the past, terror did not descend upon you from the skies out of nothingness. Wars always are conspired in secret and loosed upon the people on Terra with noble slogans, and so you agree to fight and die without complaints. What nation can ever justly claim that it started a holy war or a war of liberation? History refutes such fantasies. Wars are inevitably fought out of self-imposed fear, hatred, greed for riches, conquest, man-made exaltation or madness. And yet there has never been a nation on Terra which did not shout for peace and not for war, for liberty and not for slavery. You have cried this through the ages, and still cry, and there lies the seed of your universal death. This evil one gives you the heroic words that lead to your destruction; it is he who arms you. But some of you deny him. Now see for yourselves of his true existence. We must all pray now. Pray for the planet to be safe from this devilish war. Even you, who have never known prayer, repeat after me... Creator, please protect us, your children, from this awful death." The entire planet of Terra in the main cities received this broadcast. The masses watched in horror and fear as the six brothers stood side by side and metamorphosed into their original penguin forms. They then metamorphosed back to human form. They all then spoke in the language of all of Terra. Everyone could interpret Michael's speech. A miracle in itself. The people of Terra who received the broadcast followed Michael's instructions and knelt and prayed the small prayer to the Creator for their survival.

Hanael and his brothers brought the main television cameras out onto Tiananmen Square and focused it towards the stage. They went back to the mansion, knowing that they had to deal with David Penn and his evil.

All the ceremonial functions were in place. Hanael's adoption was going smoothly. Hanael knew that after his adoption there was going to be the most extraordinary deliverance of mankind that Terra had ever experienced.

The Central Military Commission of China decided to release the nuclear warheads during the adoption. Tiananmen Square at 6 in the morning was a sea of vast humanity. The adoption was to take place in an hour. David Penn did not sleep at all the night before. He plotted with the minds of the Communist Chinese government that they would be the leaders of the entire Terra if they pushed the buttons necessary for the nuclear disaster. He knew he had them almost completely convinced it was the only thing to do to save the dignity of China.

At 7 am, Pu-Linn, Yu-Chen, Hanael and his brothers and their fathers walked onto the stage in Tiananmen Square. There was a microphone in the center of the stage. Pu-Linn walked up to it and announced, "Thank you all for honoring me and my family at this most historic moment. My wife, Yu-Chen and I have been blessed with a son. We would like to introduce you to Hanael." Hanael took center stage at the microphone. He looked around and finally spotted David. With a penetrating stare, Hanael looked directly at David and announced, "My brothers of China, I have been selected to bring peace and love to your country. In the same manner, my brothers here brought peace and love to their country which the Creator chose while we were still on the planet Pellisa. The Creator is the Father of all of us, every Terra living creature, all the planets of your Universe and all the various species living on the other planets of 400 billion galaxies, including Pellisa. I am from the oldest galaxy and Terra is a planet from the youngest, therefore my planet is far more advanced than yours. We have not sinned so we have no death. We were sent here to bring love and peace and stop the murdering and slaughtering which takes place over Terra. All of you should turn to the Creator and ask Him to bring peace amongst you. There is an evil one that has tempted all of you through the generations. He is concerned only with the destruction of Terra. Have faith that all will be united by the love we have for one another. Believe in a brotherhood of all men and reject none. The harmony will return to all who live on Terra if this is done. I would now like to introduce David Penn, the magician who will entertain us with his most incredible magic tricks."

David walked up to the stage totally horrified. The force he could feel coming from Hanael and his brothers made David light-headed. He shook hands with Hanael and stepped up to the microphone. David proceeded to say, "Thank you, Hanael, and congratulations on your adoption. This is surely a historical day. I wish to thank Pu-Linn for inviting me, it is truly an honor. I always felt the Chinese culture was the oldest living today and, for this reason, the Chinese should rule Terra. They should never stand for anyone interfering with their private government. Anyone who does so should be punished." The crowd, having heard Hanael's speech stating the opposite, became quite confused, which was David's intention. Hanael knew David would contradict him, so Hanael walked up to David and said, "David, I'm Chinese. My brothers here on the stage are all of different nationalities, yet we are all the same." David looked at Hanael and said, "Prove it." Hanael, Michael, Raphael, Gabriel, Uriel and Jophiel all held hands and rubbed their gold rings. Their garments started ripping and their shoes split in half. Their white and gold penguin fur covered their bodies and they were in full penguin form. The crowds became silent. David Penn knew he was in big trouble. All of the penguins formed a circle around David. They all asked him to repent and ask the Creator for forgiveness. David was trapped. He said to them, "The Creator made me, Lucifer, more magnificent, more glorious in light, most noble of countenance, so endowed with beauty and subtlety, so puissant in word and deed, so brilliant of eye and strong of masculine voice, so fearless, so full of laughter and humor. None of you penguins from Pellisa come close to me, nor can any other being." "Ah, but you Lucifer," replied Hanael, "continue to fall away from our Creator, and each step you fall again through the offices of men." Lucifer became furious and replied, "Beautiful vast worlds of blinding color and enormous vistas and splendid cities, and with men who could at least claim to have a wink of the intelligence I have known on other worlds, but this one revolts me with her half desert, half storm, half polluted seas, and half eroded mountains. It is a fit habitat of the creature which reared itself on his hind legs and dared to call itself a man!"

The six penguin brothers were aware that the crowd was very

confused. David Penn's true identity needed to be revealed. They asked all who knew how to pray to do so, then all six touched David's shoulders and told him to reveal himself. David concentrated on his satanic army. He mentally ordered them to descend upon the clouds. As they came forward in droves, the Beijing sky became dark as night. Then, within seconds, the sound of a trumpet was so overpowering everyone held their ears. The population of Terra watching around the earth became so frightened. No matter what country they lived in, they too experienced the sound of the trumpet. On one side of the sky, Satan's army lined the heavens in the darkness. As the trumpet became louder, the brightest beam of light started shining through the dark clouds. As this light grew closer to Terra, it was clear to see there were figures of angels descending with it. The inhabitants of Terra watched in wondrous awe as the light began to brighten up the sky. Approaching on a cloud appeared the Creator in brilliant light. The trumpet was carried by an angel who stood at the middle of the sky between the good and evil armies. The sound of the trumpet stopped and the angel announced, "The Creator again has sent these, his prophets, to your Terra, only now whoever did not follow the warning of the six penguin prophets to love one another will have to pay the price of evil. What army have you chosen to follow? Where have you destined your soul for all eternity? Hold the hands of your fellow human next to you and ask the Creator to forgive you for any injustices you may have committed towards your human family."

The Creator spoke to David, "There has been a universal prayer of forgiveness from these humans. The entire Terra has prayed together for peace. I now have my children back. They are now willing to love one another regardless of their differences. Therefore, they have stopped this nuclear devastation. It is up to you now, Lucifer, to save yourself from the eternal damnation brought upon you. Kneel down and ask for My forgiveness."

Lucifer could not believe how successfully the penguin prophets brought together this planet he hated. He felt pain for all his deception toward humanity. He finally saw they were competent to heal themselves because of a love and understanding of each other.

Crying tears of joy, Lucifer knelt down and cried, "Forgive me, my Creator, I now see how holy and loving humanity can be. You have loved them all along. Now I see their good and will kneel at your feet and ask for forgiveness." And with that, the nuclear holocaust was halted and love and peace came upon all of Terra, and Satan was defeated for all of eternity.

ACKNOWLEDGMENTS

My Thanks goes to Thomas M for his support and contribution and belief in this story and his love.

Allen K my wonderful, talented family member in contributing the cover art. Also to my loyal family and friends who heard about my penguin book for thirty five years: Chris, Vikki, Gloria and Rhonda-Pearl.

ABOUT THE AUTHOR

Elizabeth is a messenger bringing the message of world peace.

www.ingramcontent.com/pod-product-compliance
Lightning Source LLC
Chambersburg PA
CBHW050421110726
47899CB00008B/2797